Drawing Vertical Lines

Name

To parents: W... ...e drawing exercises help your child to develop basic pencil-control skills. Have your child draw lines carefully. When your child completes each exercise, praise him or her.

■ Draw a line from top to bottom connecting the two pictures.

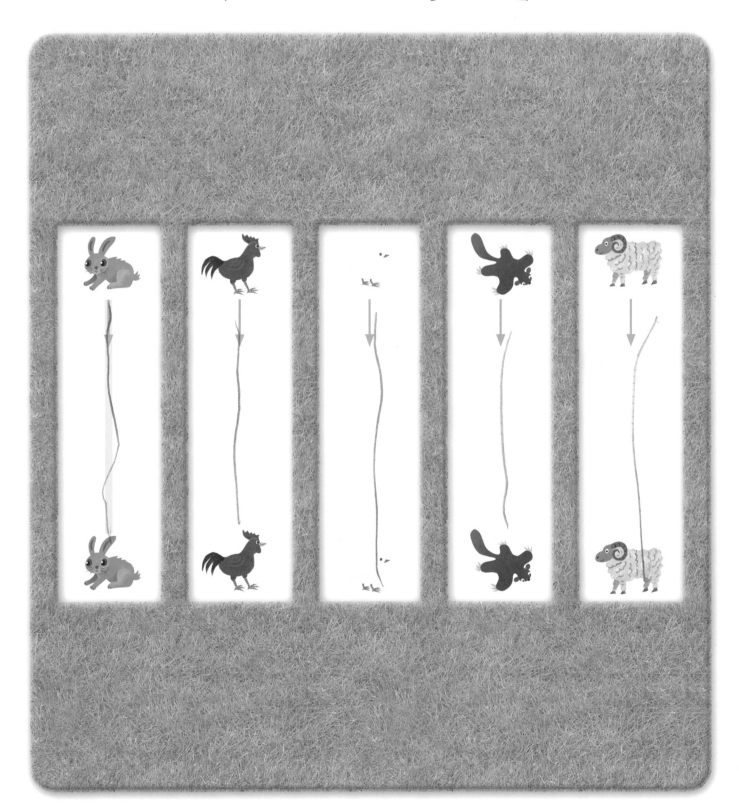

■ Draw a line from top to bottom connecting the two pictures.

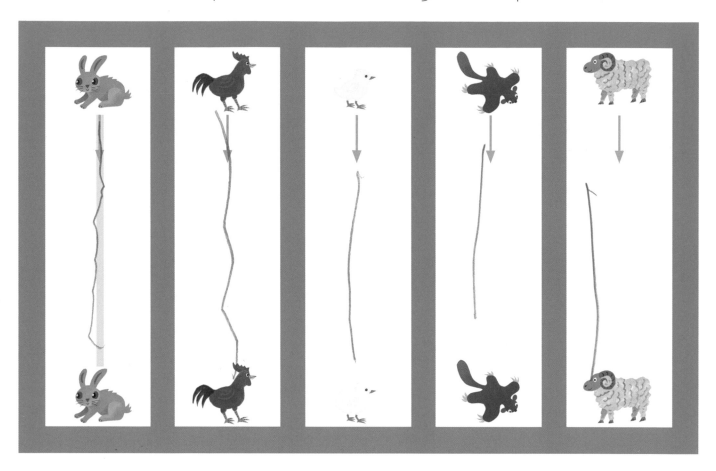

Drawing Horizontal Lines

Name

Date

/ / /

To parents: It is okay if your child draws outside the white area. The important thing is to encourage your child to draw slowly and carefully.

■ Draw a line from left to right connecting the two pictures.

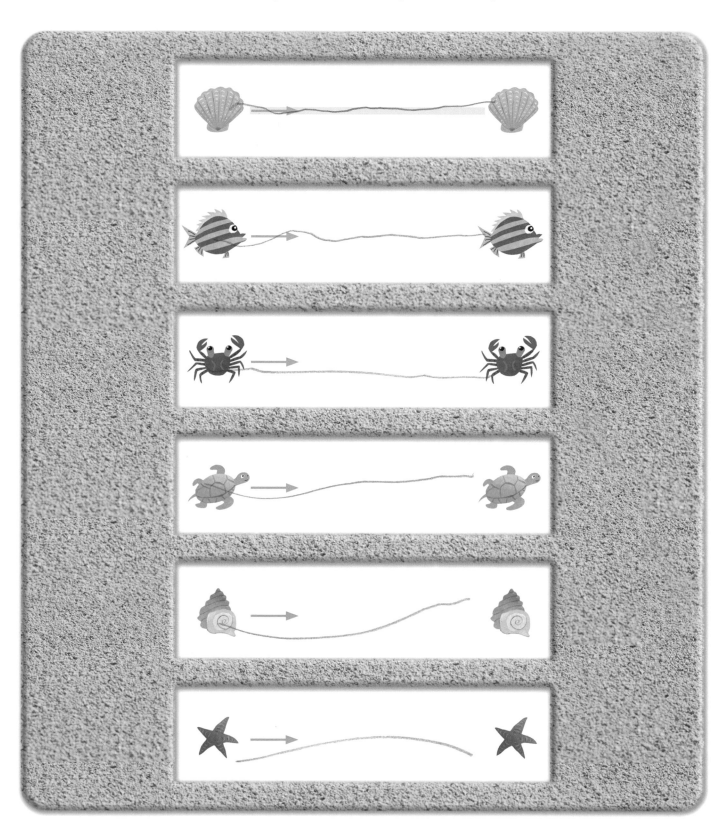

■ Draw a line from left to right connecting the two pictures.

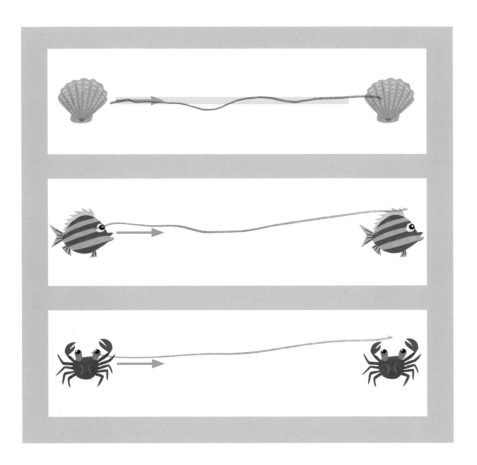

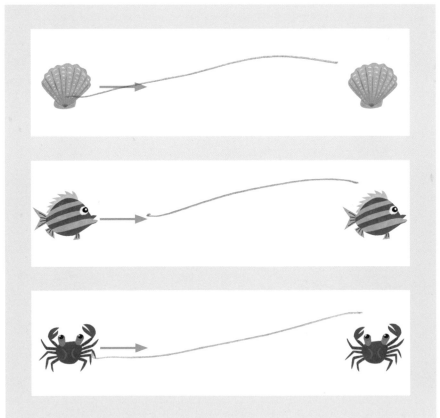

3 Drawing Bending Lines

Name

Date

/ /

To parents: Make sure your child stops the pencil at each corner before drawing in a new direction. When your child has finished, offer praise, such as "Great job!"

■ Draw a line from top to bottom connecting the two pictures.

■ Draw a line from left to right connecting the two pictures.

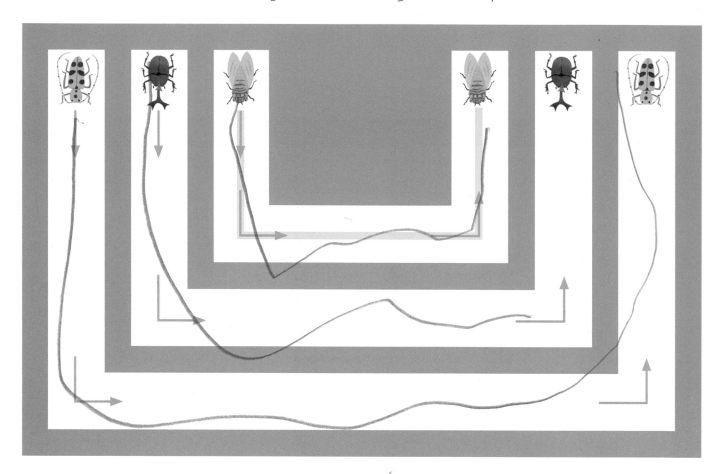

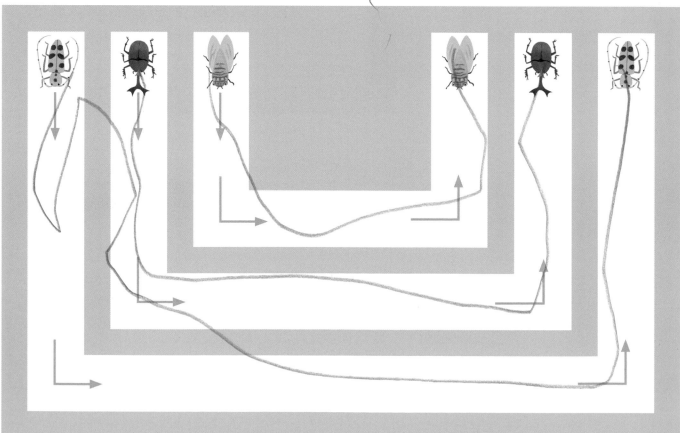

Name

Date
/ /

To parents: Before your child begins writing, please read the words on the page and ask your child to repeat the words after you. If your child can recognize the letters, it might be fun to have him or her tell you the name of each letter, and to have your child say the sound of the letter aloud while he or she traces it. If your child is still learning the alphabet, you should tell him or her the name of the letter and teach him or her its sound while tracing.

■ Draw a line from the dot(●) to the star(★).

A B C D E F G H I J K **L** M N O P Q R S T U V W X Y Z

Writing T

■ Draw a line from the dot(●) to the star(★).
  Follow the order of the numbers.

T TOMATO

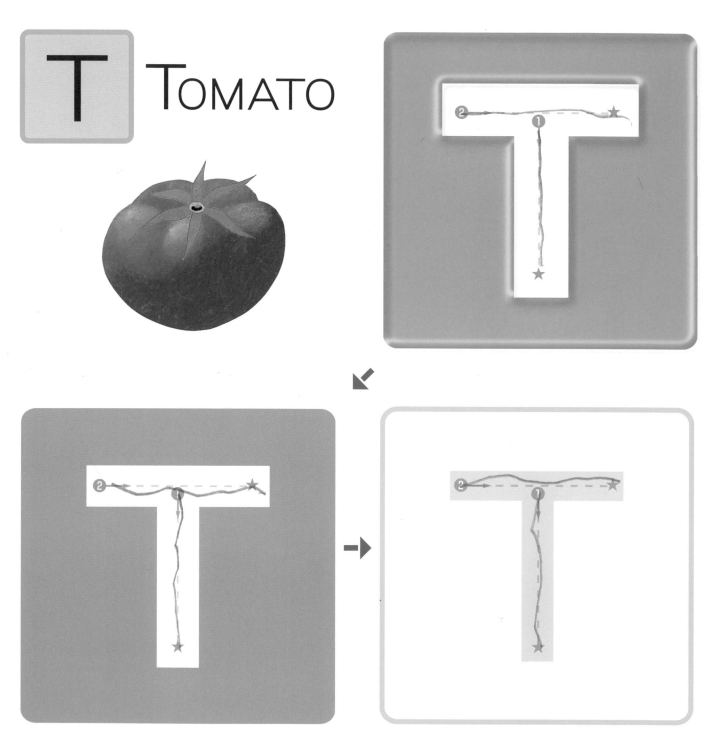

| A | B | C | D | E | F | G | H | I | J | K | L | M | N | O | P | Q | R | S | T | U | V | W | X | Y | Z |

Name

Date

/ /

■ Draw a line from the dot(●) to the star(★).
Follow the order of the numbers.

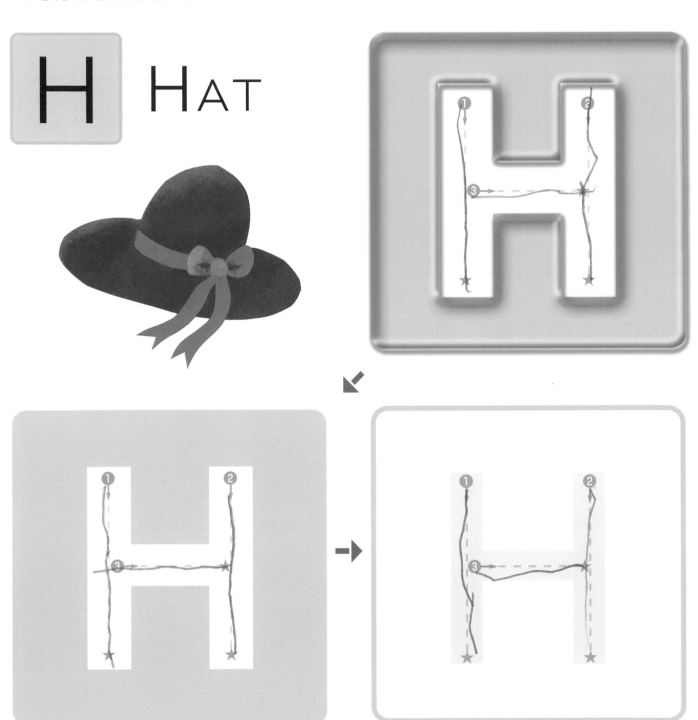

H HAT

A B C D E F G H I J K L M N O P Q R S T U V W X Y Z

Writing L, T, and H

To parents: On this page, your child will practice uppercase letters again. Try to write each letter as he or she pronounces it. It is also good to have him or her try reading the English words while looking at the illustrations.

■ Draw a line from the dot(●) to the star(★).
  Follow the order of the numbers.

L IONS   T OMATO   H AT

■ Draw a line from the dot(●) to the star(★).
Follow the order of the numbers.

 **I**  **I**CE CREAM

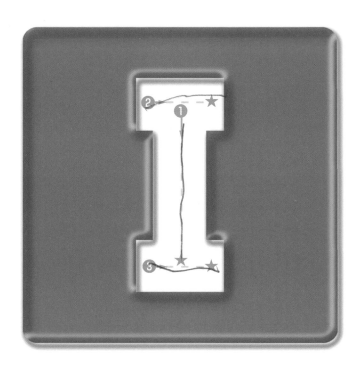

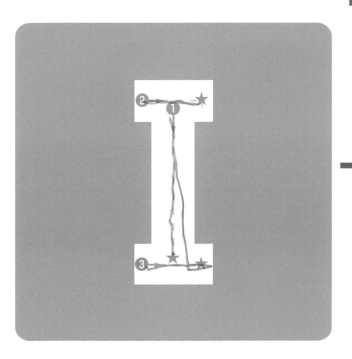 →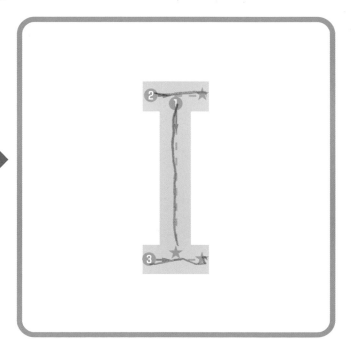

A B C D E F G H **I** J K L M N O P Q R S T U V W X Y Z

Writing F

■ Draw a line from the dot(●) to the star(★).
  Follow the order of the numbers.

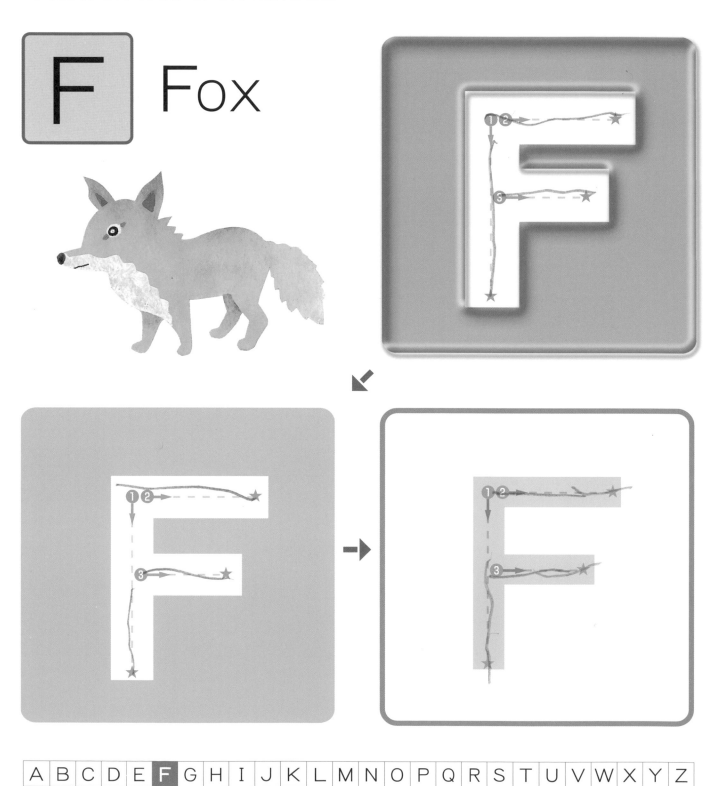

F Fox

| A | B | C | D | E | F | G | H | I | J | K | L | M | N | O | P | Q | R | S | T | U | V | W | X | Y | Z |

Name

Date

■ Draw a line from the dot(●) to the star(★).
Follow the order of the numbers.

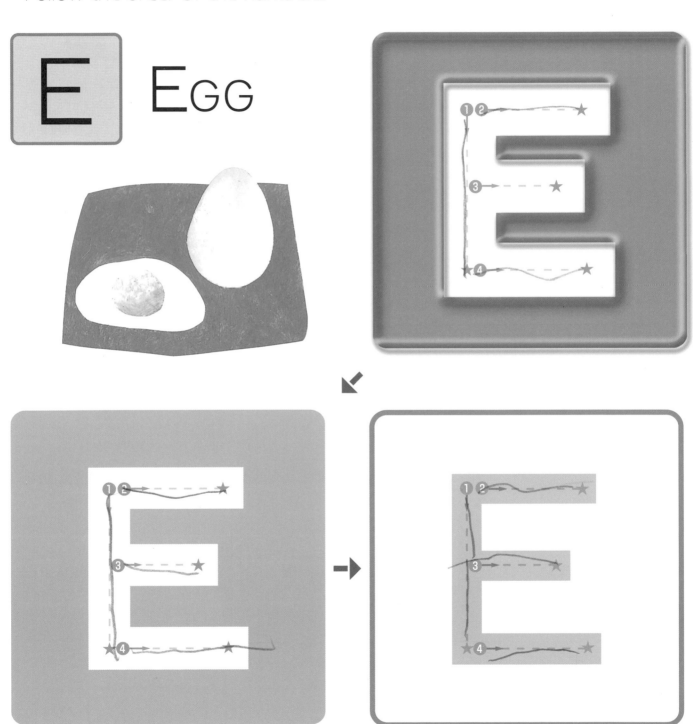

E Egg

A B C D **E** F G H I J K L M N O P Q R S T U V W X Y Z

Writing I, F, and E

■ Draw a line from the dot(●) to the star(★).
Follow the order of the numbers.

I CE CREAM   F OX   E GG

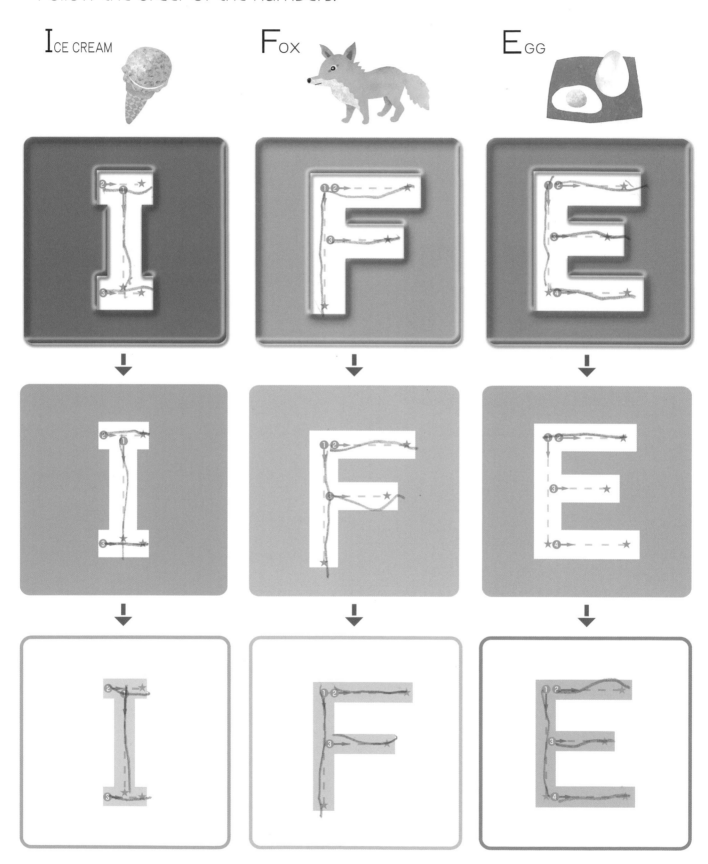

To parents: Your child will practice the uppercase letters again. In the third exercise on this page, the numbers in the stroke order and the notation of ● and ★ are slightly different from the previous exercises in order to write the alphabet more neatly. It is good to read the letters out loud after you finish writing them.

■ Draw a line from the dot(●) to the star(★).
Follow the order of the numbers.

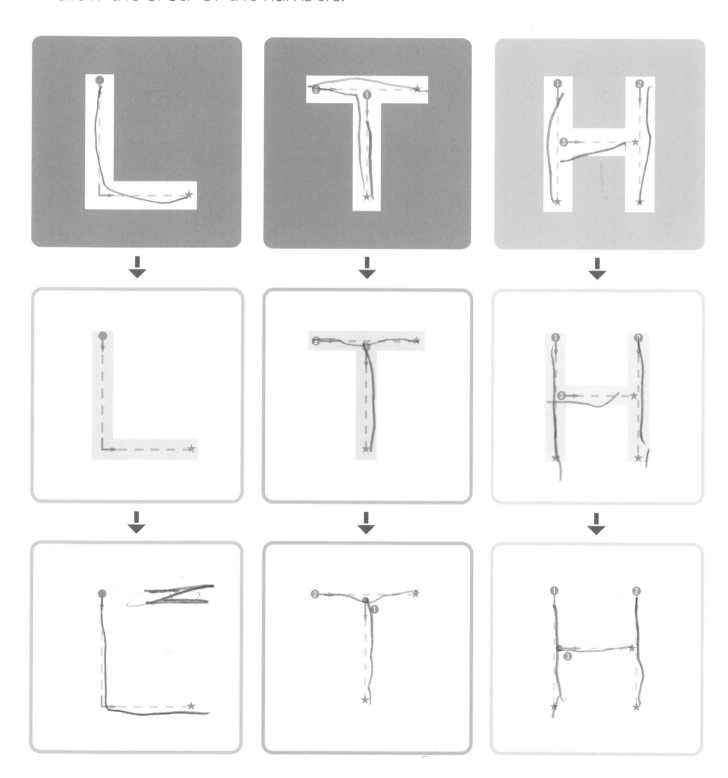

Writing I, F, and E

■ Draw a line from the dot(●) to the star(★).
  Follow the order of the numbers.

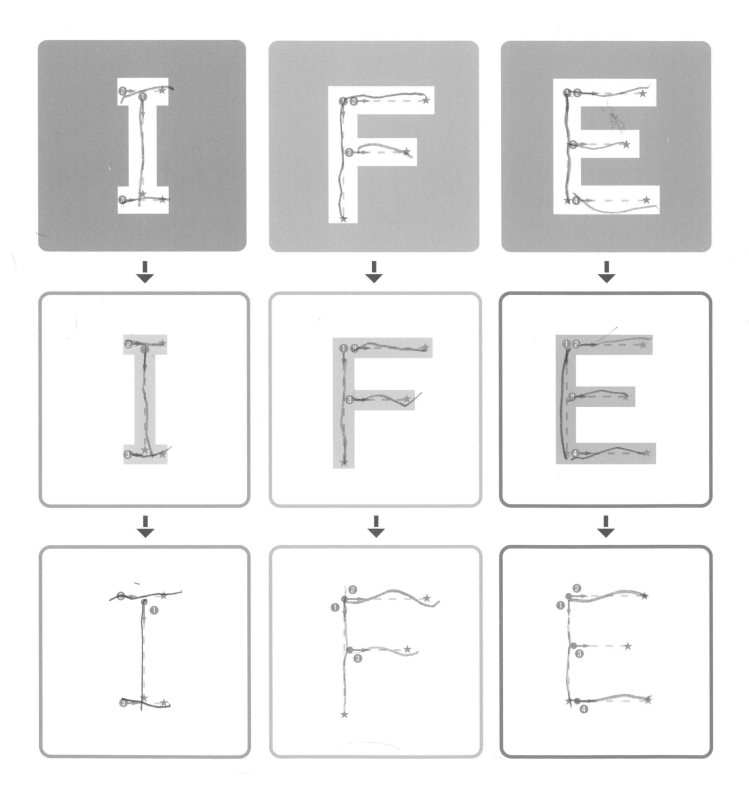

Drawing Diagonal Lines and Jagged Lines

To parents: From this page on, your child will practice drawing diagonal lines and jagged lines that will make up the letters. If your child had difficulty, you can lightly hold his or her hand as he or she draws the lines.

■ Draw a line connecting each pair of pictures.

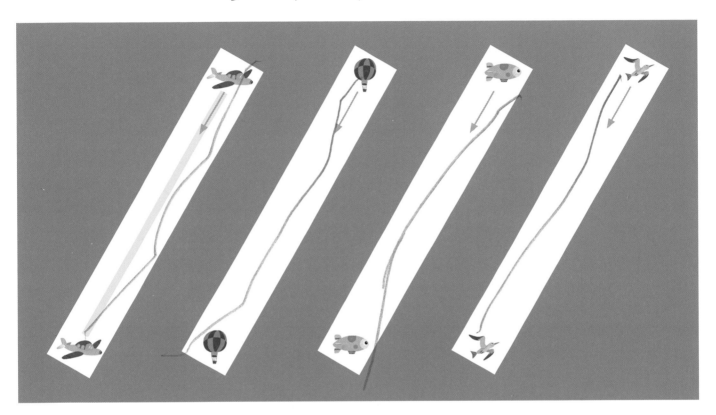

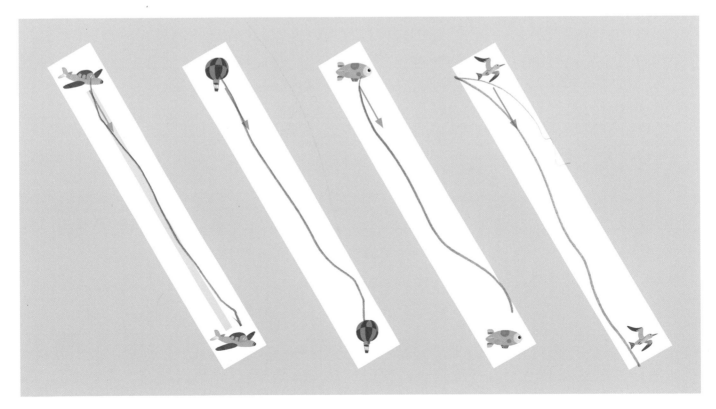

■ Draw a line connecting each pair of pictures.

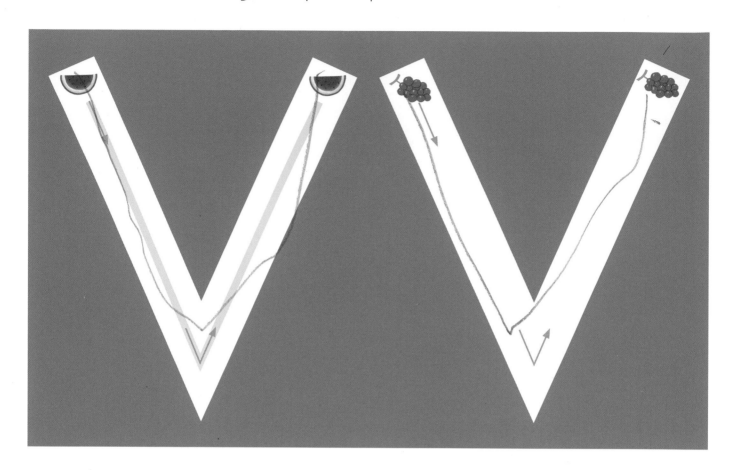

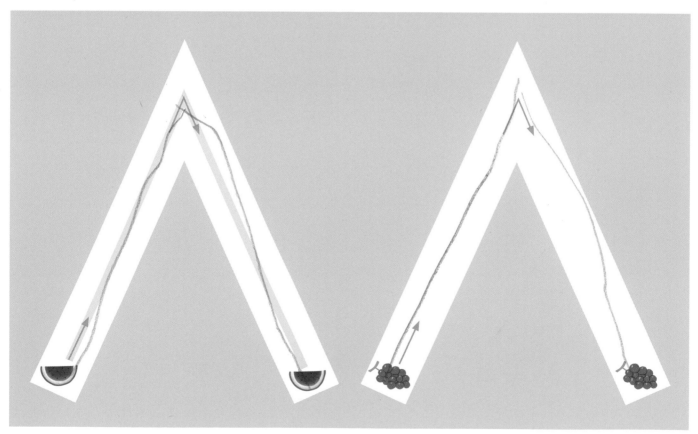

Drawing Jagged Lines

To parents: Drawing jagged lines can be difficult for children. It is a good idea to use colored pencils or crayons and practice drawing them over and over again in different colors.

■ Draw a line connecting each pair of pictures.

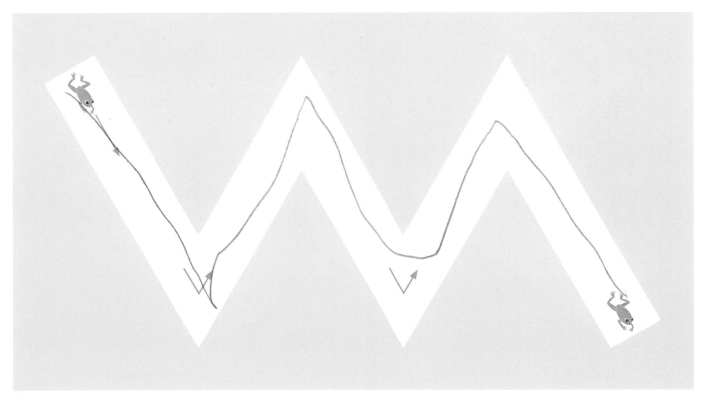

■ Draw a line connecting each pair of pictures.

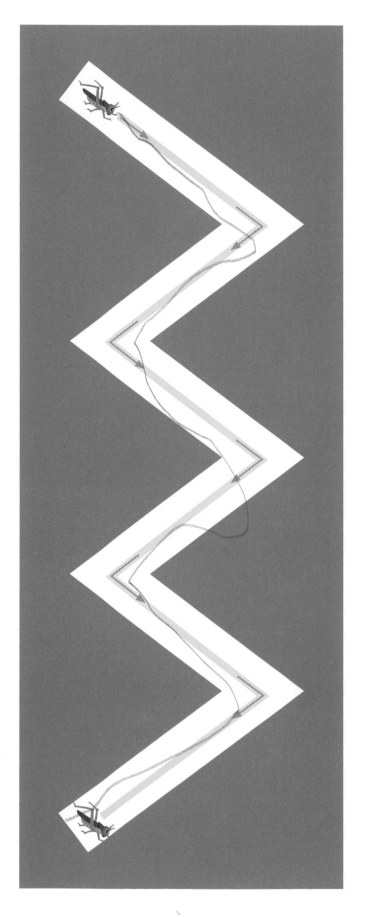

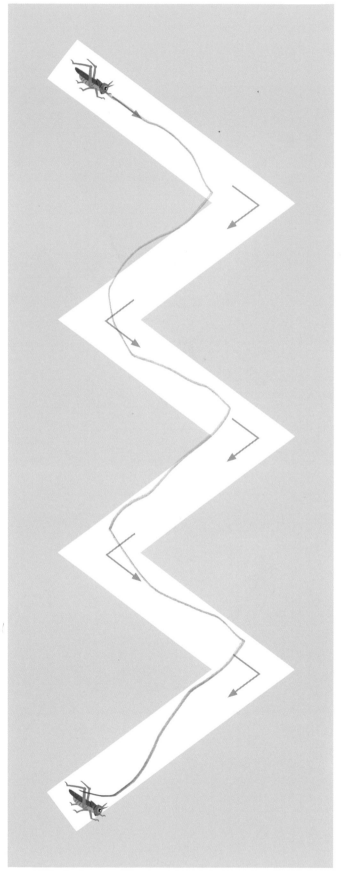

Name

Date

/ /

■ Draw a line from the dot(●) to the star(★).
Follow the order of the numbers.

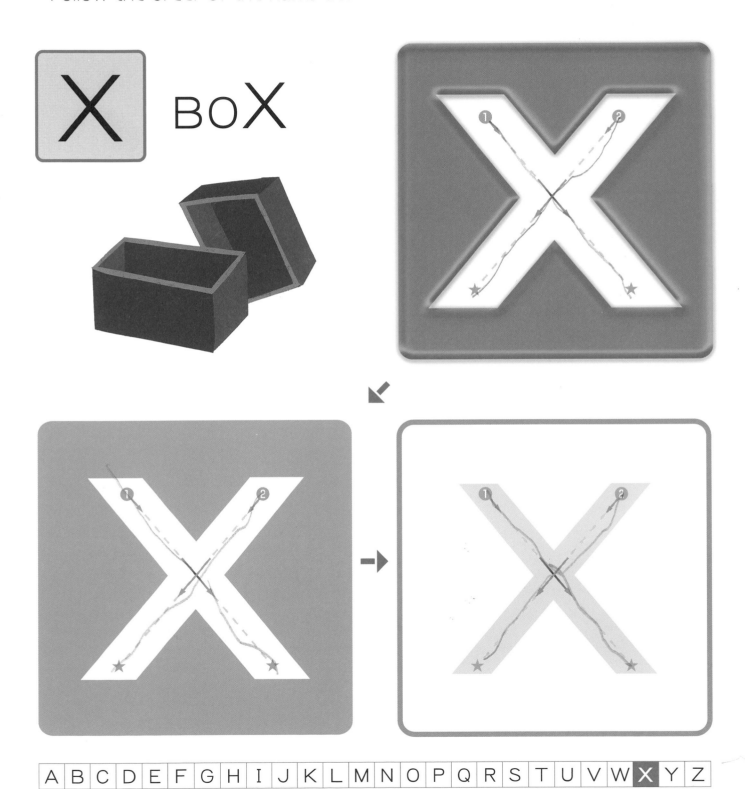

X BOX

| A | B | C | D | E | F | G | H | I | J | K | L | M | N | O | P | Q | R | S | T | U | V | W | X | Y | Z |

Writing V

■ Draw a line from the dot(●) to the star(★).

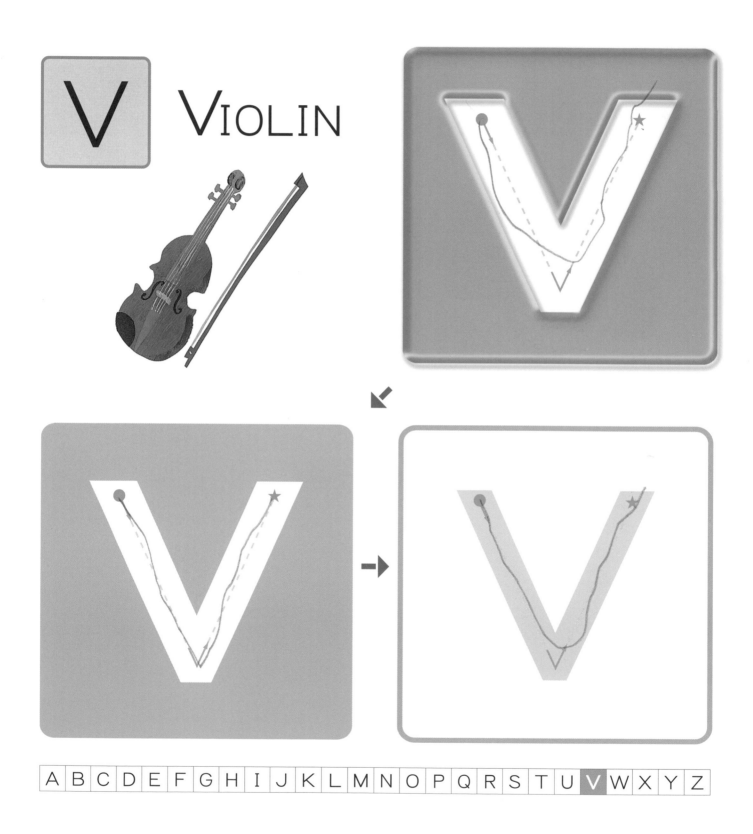

| A | B | C | D | E | F | G | H | I | J | K | L | M | N | O | P | Q | R | S | T | U | V | W | X | Y | Z |

■ Draw a line from the dot(●) to the star(★).
  Follow the order of the numbers.

Y YACHT

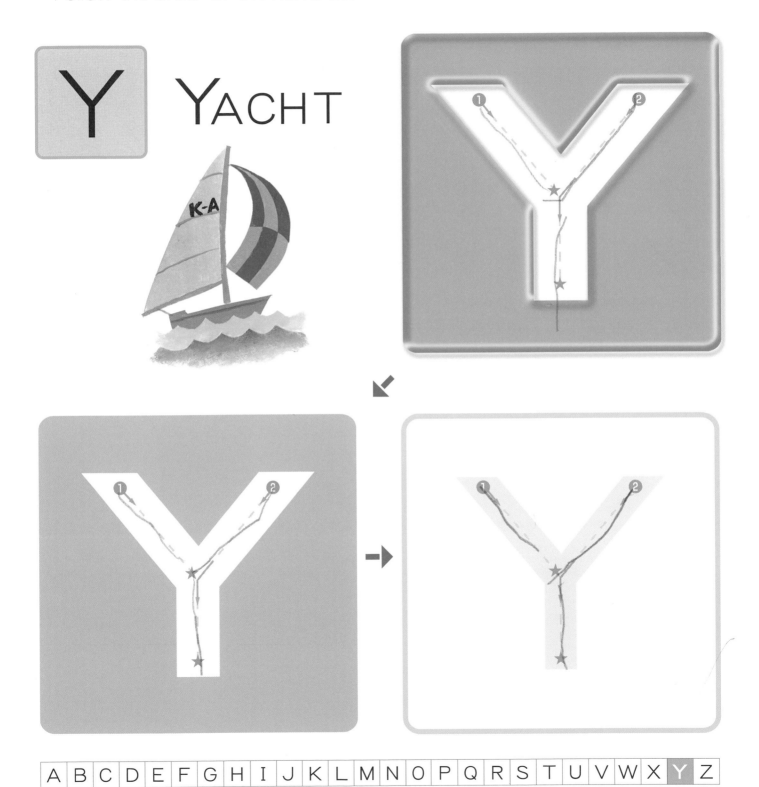

A B C D E F G H I J K L M N O P Q R S T U V W X Y Z

Writing X, V, and Y

■ Draw a line from the dot(●) to the star(★).
Follow the order of the numbers.

BO**X** VIOLIN YACHT

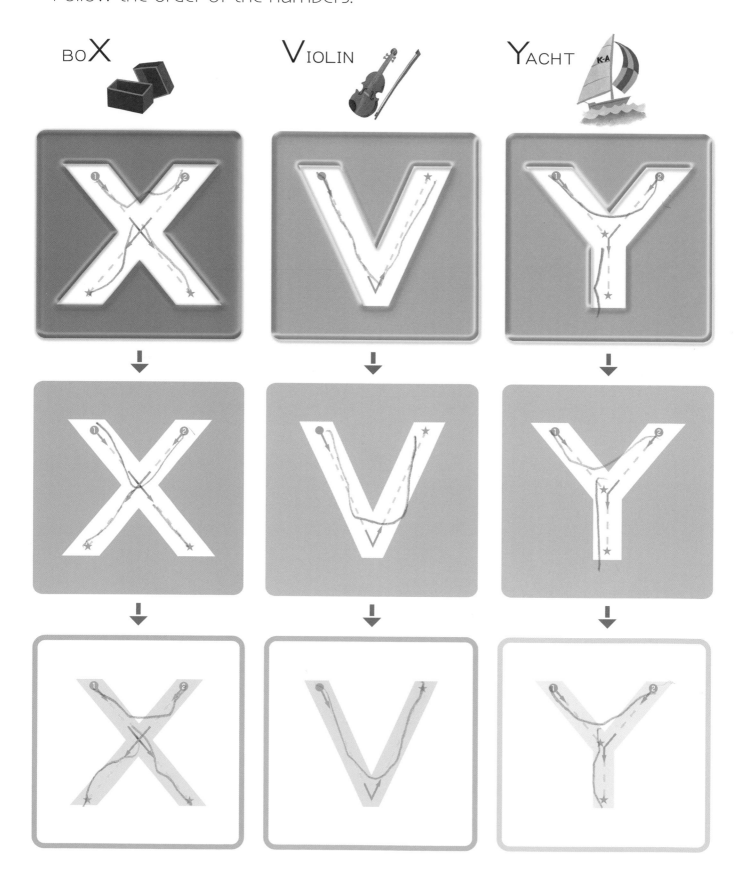

Name

Date   /   /

■ Draw a line from the dot(●) to the star(★).
Follow the order of the numbers.

N NOSE

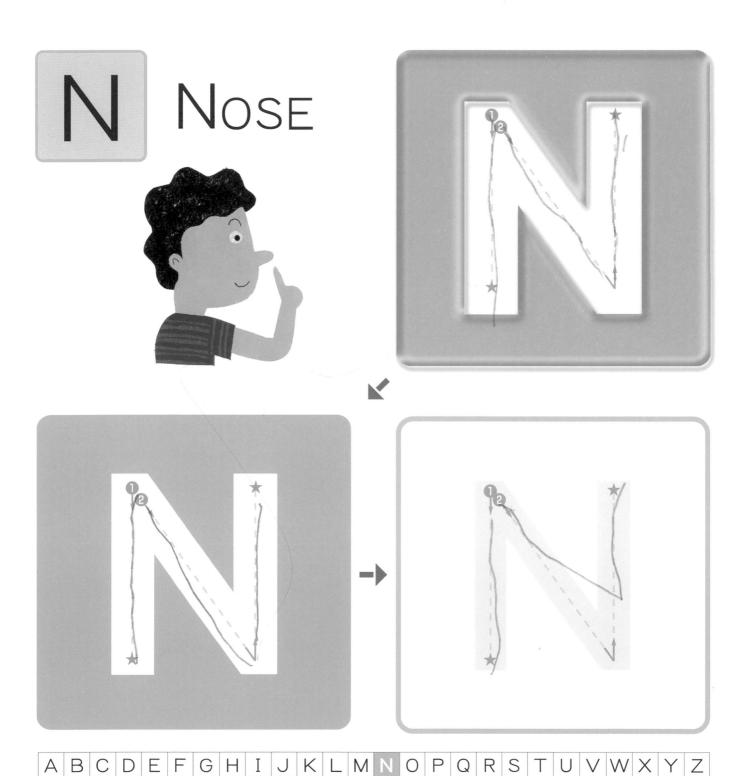

A B C D E F G H I J K L M N O P Q R S T U V W X Y Z

Writing Z

■ Draw a line from the dot(●) to the star(★).

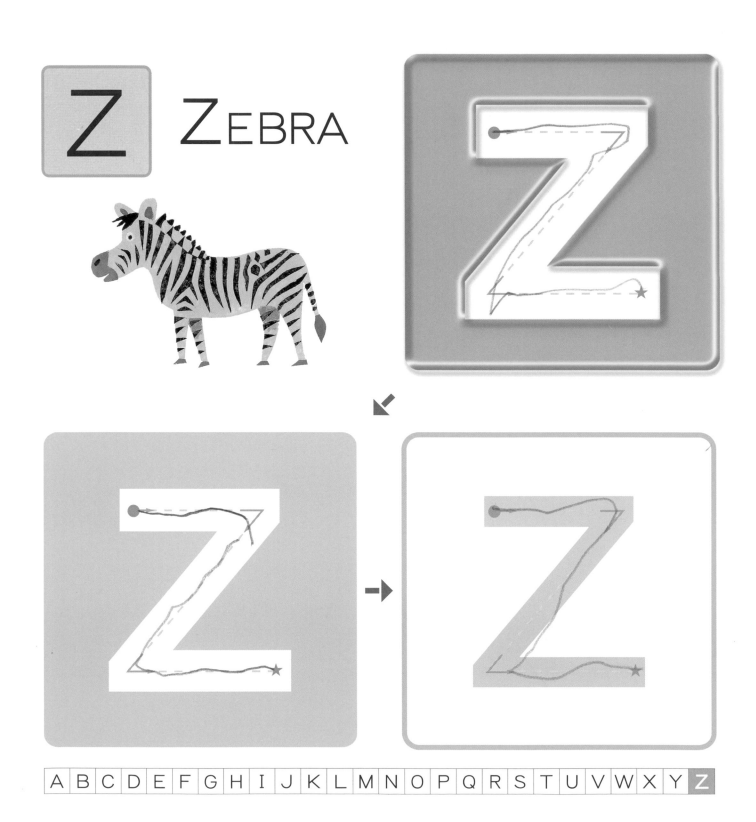

Z ZEBRA

| A | B | C | D | E | F | G | H | I | J | K | L | M | N | O | P | Q | R | S | T | U | V | W | X | Y | Z |

Name

Date

■ Draw a line from the dot(●) to the star(★).
Follow the order of the numbers.

A APPLE

A B C D E F G H I J K L M N O P Q R S T U V W X Y Z

Writing N, Z, and A

■ Draw a line from the dot(●) to the star(★).
Follow the order of the numbers.

NOSE ZEBRA APPLE

Name

Date / /

■ Draw a line from the dot(●) to the star(★).
Follow the order of the numbers.

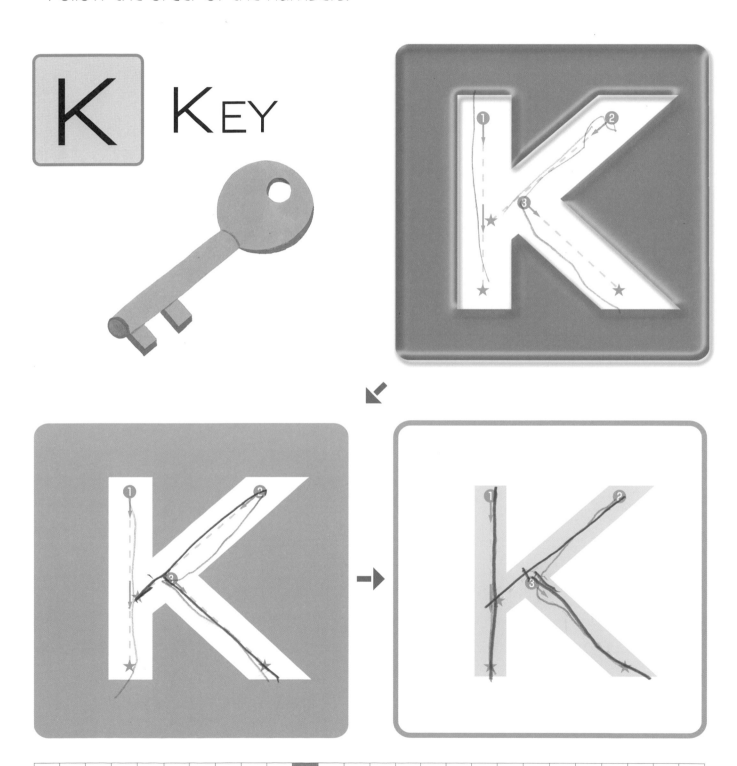

K KEY

A B C D E F G H I J **K** L M N O P Q R S T U V W X Y Z

Writing M

■ Draw a line from the dot(●) to the star(★).
Follow the order of the numbers.

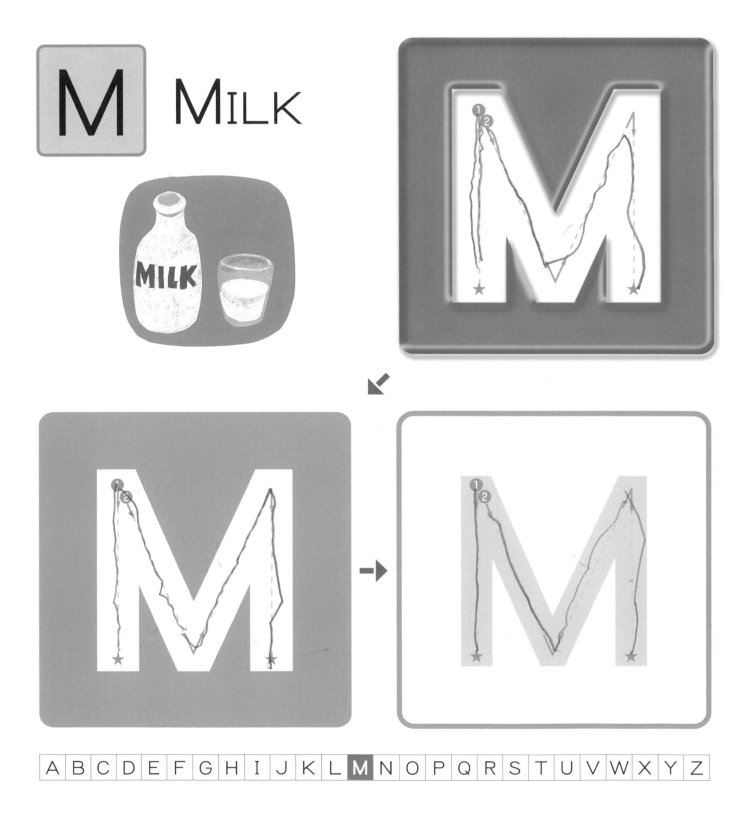

| A | B | C | D | E | F | G | H | I | J | K | L | **M** | N | O | P | Q | R | S | T | U | V | W | X | Y | Z |

■ Draw a line from the dot(●) to the star(★).

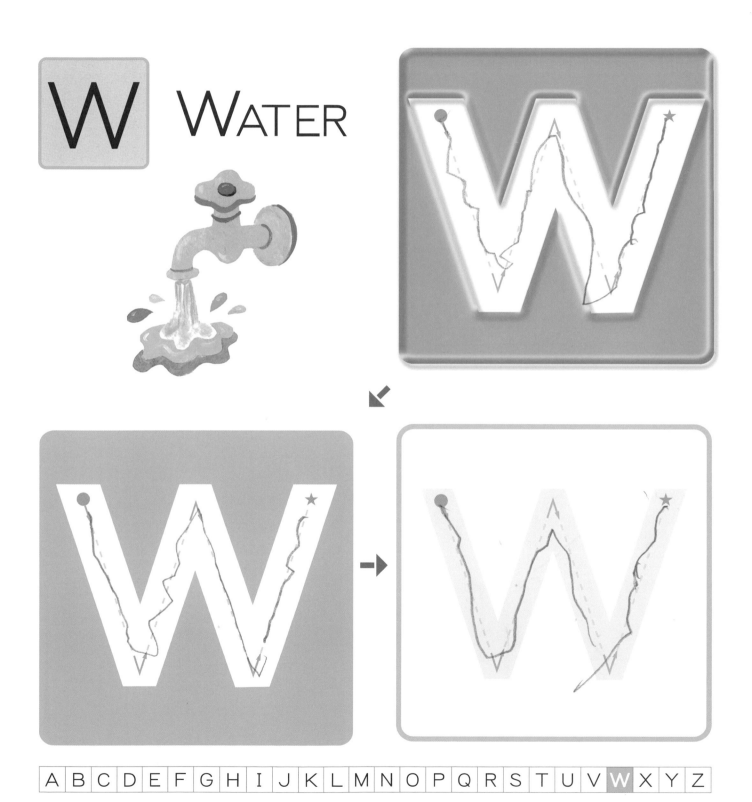

W WATER

Writing K, M, and W

■ Draw a line from the dot (●) to the star (★).
Follow the order of the numbers.

Key Milk Water

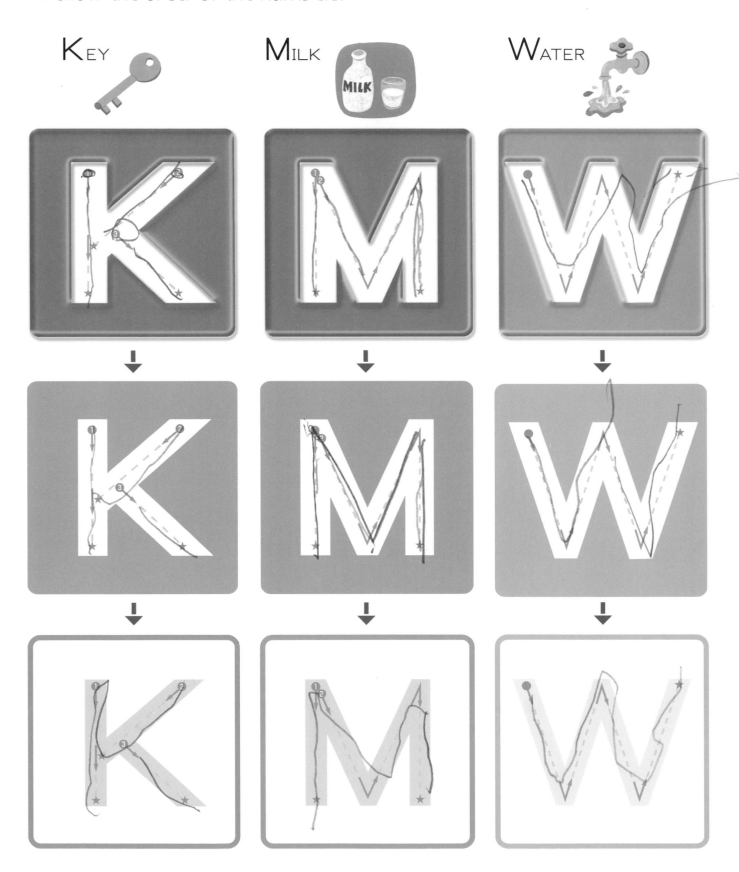

Name   Date

To parents: It is good to have your child say the letters out loud after he or she finishes writing them. When your child has completed the exercise, offer a lot of praise.

■ Draw a line from the dot(●) to the star(★). Follow the order of the numbers.

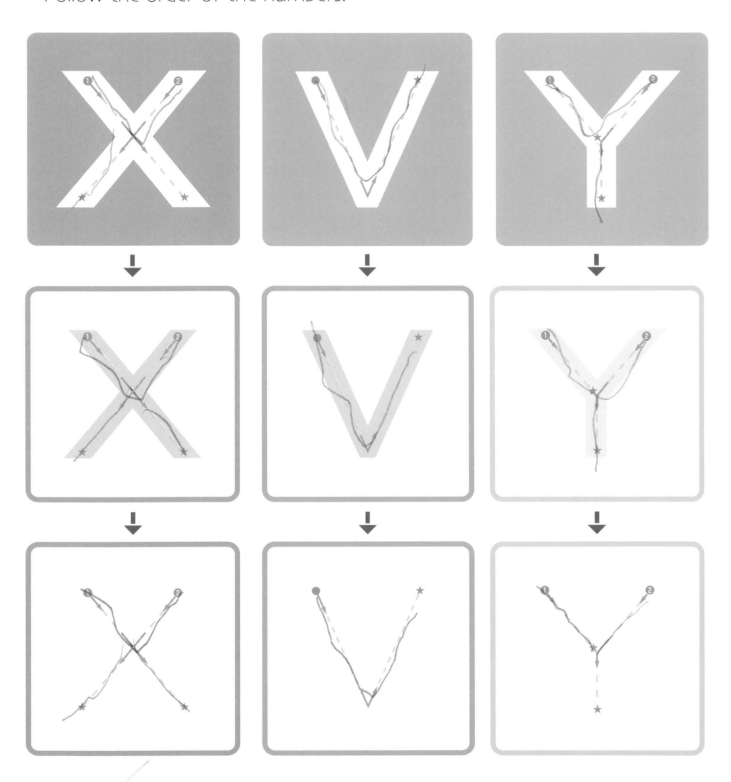

Writing N, Z, and A

■ Draw a line from the dot(●) to the star(★).
Follow the order of the numbers.

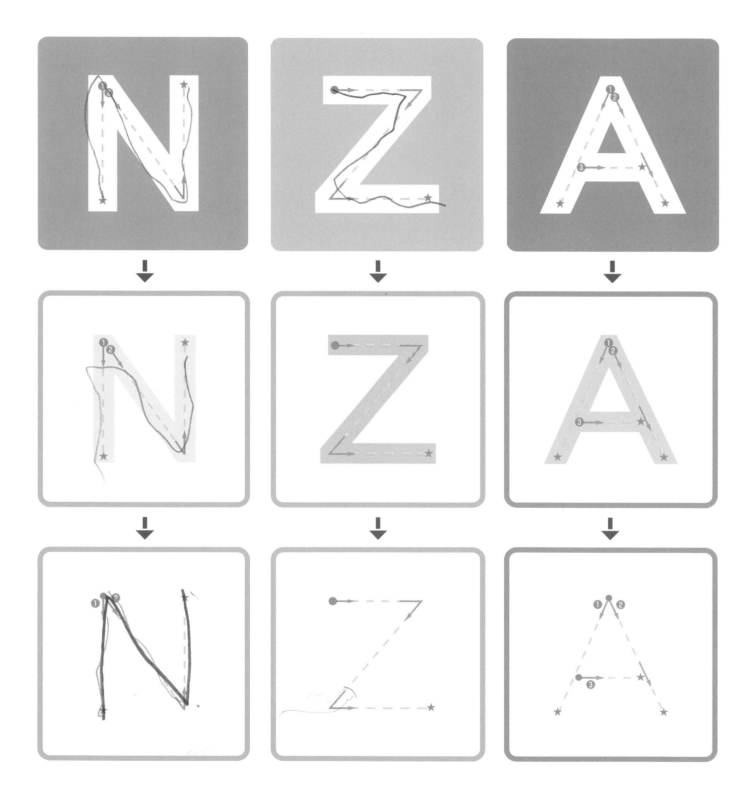

Review
Writing K, M, and W

■ Draw a line from the dot(●) to the star(★).
  Follow the order of the numbers.

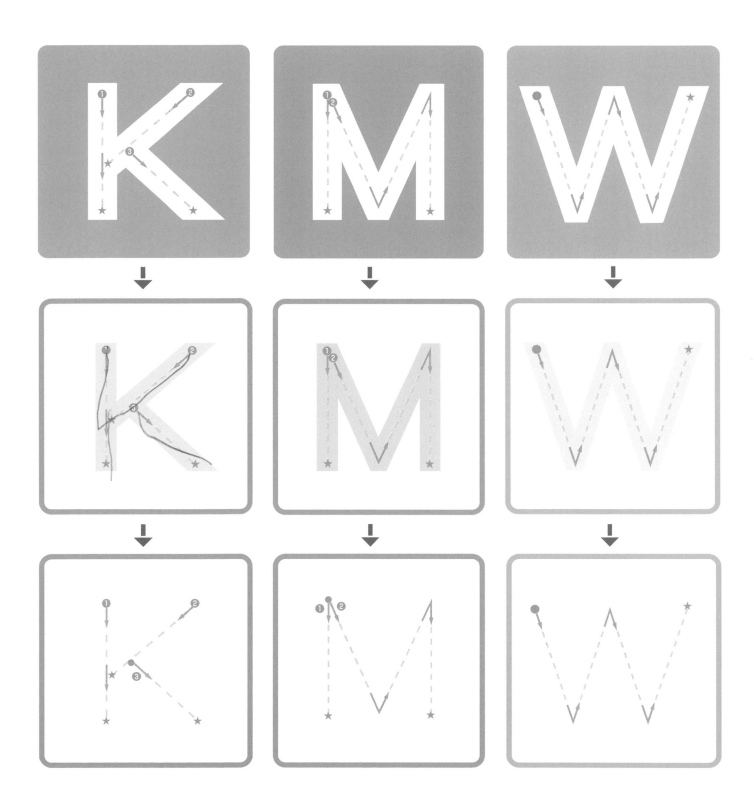

■ Trace the letters below.

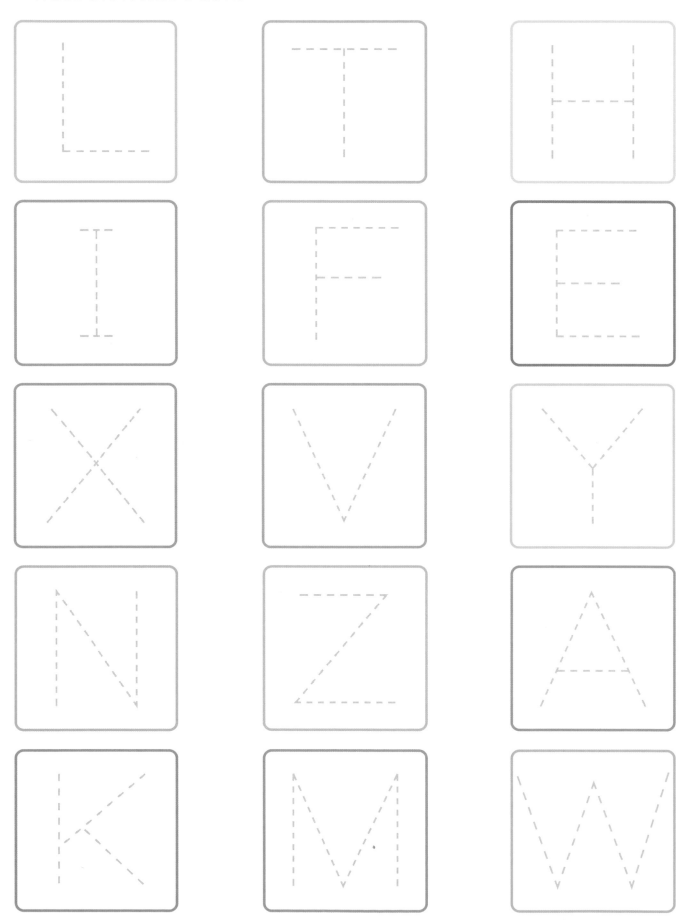

Drawing
Right Curved Lines

Name

Date

/ /

To parents: From this page on, your child will practice drawing curved lines that will make up letters. Encourage your child to move his or her pencil slowly along the curved path.

■ Draw a line connecting each pair of pictures.

■ Draw a line connecting each pair of pictures.

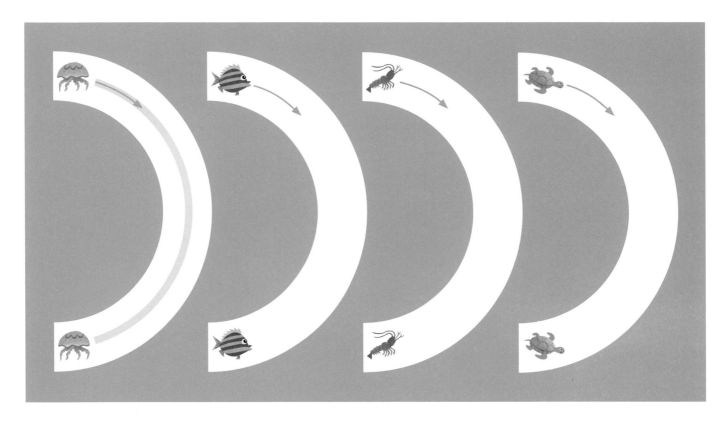

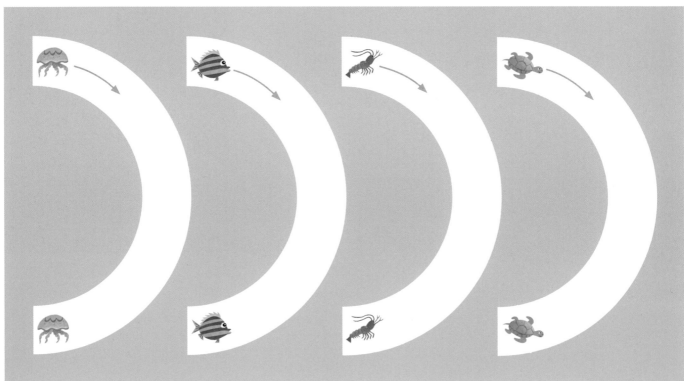

20 Drawing Left Curved Lines

■ Draw a line connecting each pair of pictures.

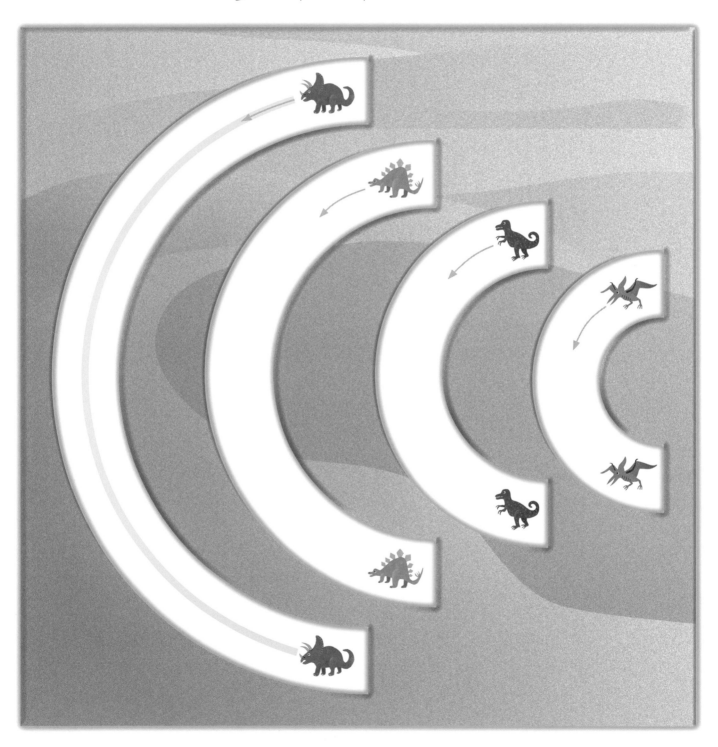

■ Draw a line connecting each pair of pictures.

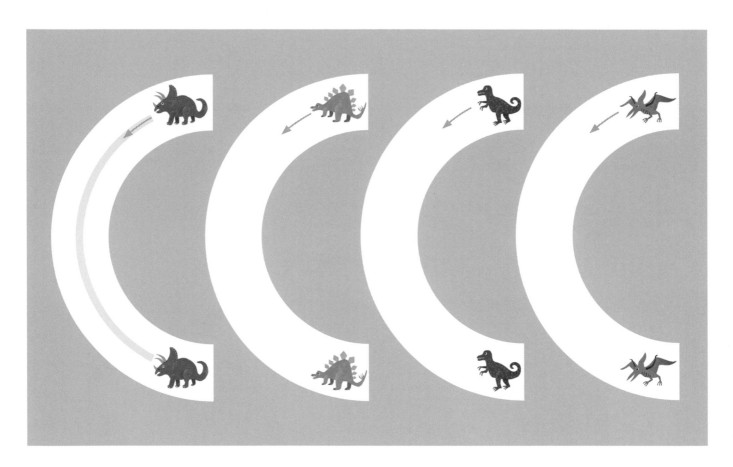

40

■ Draw a line from the dot(●) to the star(★).
Follow the order of the numbers.

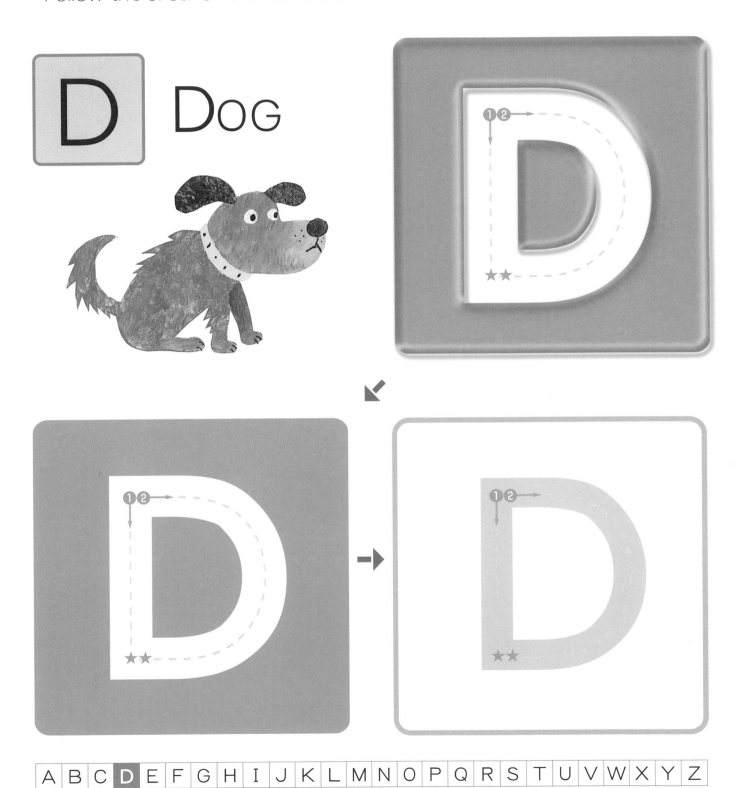

D Dog

A B C **D** E F G H I J K L M N O P Q R S T U V W X Y Z

■ Draw a line from the dot(●) to the star(★).
Follow the order of the numbers.

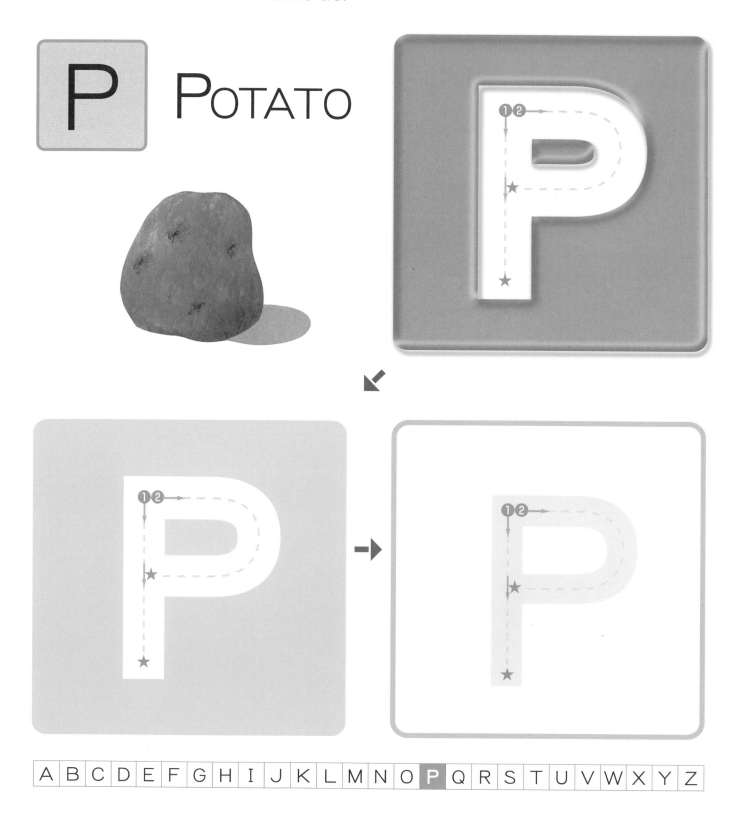

P POTATO

A B C D E F G H I J K L M N O P Q R S T U V W X Y Z

Name

Date

/ / /

■ Draw a line from the dot(●) to the star(★).
Follow the order of the numbers.

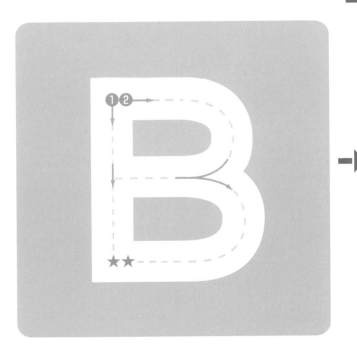 →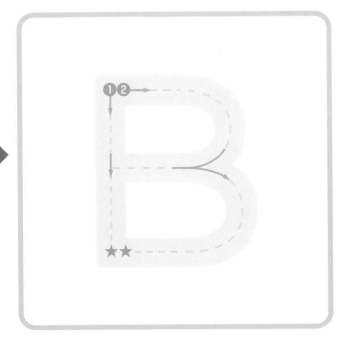

A **B** C D E F G H I J K L M N O P Q R S T U V W X Y Z

Writing D, P, and B

■ Draw a line from the dot(●) to the star(★).
Follow the order of the numbers.

Dog   Potato   Bag

■ Draw a line from the dot(●) to the star(★).
  Follow the order of the numbers.

 R RING

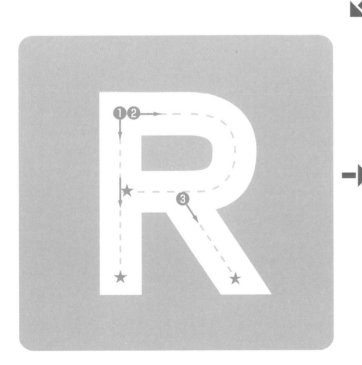

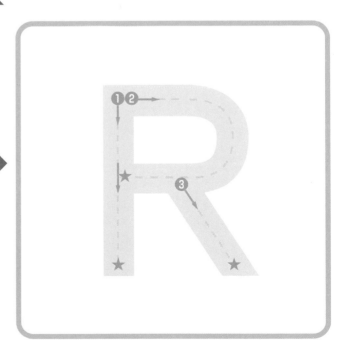

| A | B | C | D | E | F | G | H | I | J | K | L | M | N | O | P | Q | **R** | S | T | U | V | W | X | Y | Z |

Writing J

■ Draw a line from the dot(●) to the star(★).

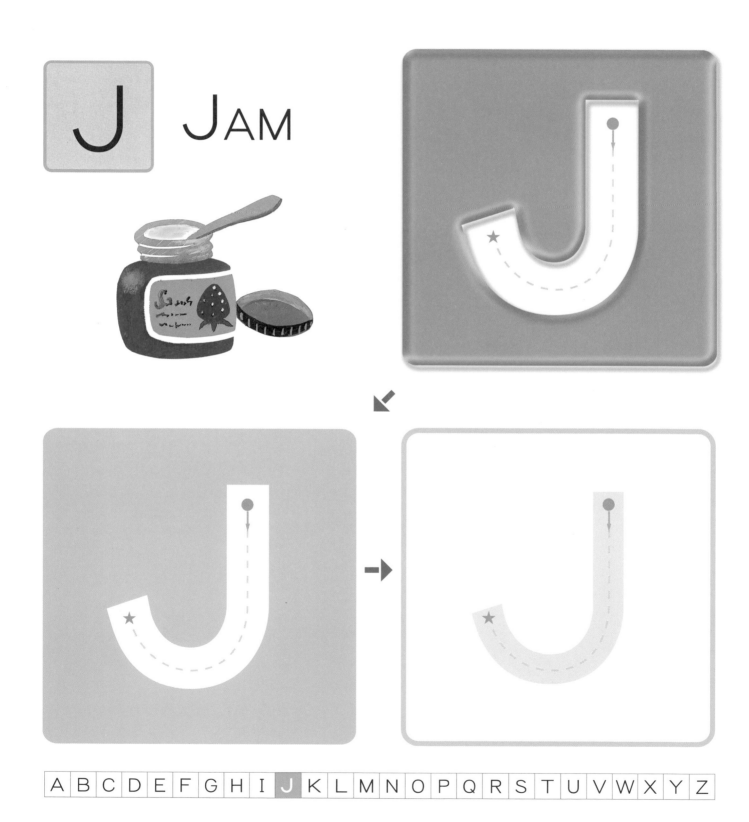

| A | B | C | D | E | F | G | H | I | J | K | L | M | N | O | P | Q | R | S | T | U | V | W | X | Y | Z |

■ Draw a line from the dot(●) to the star(★).

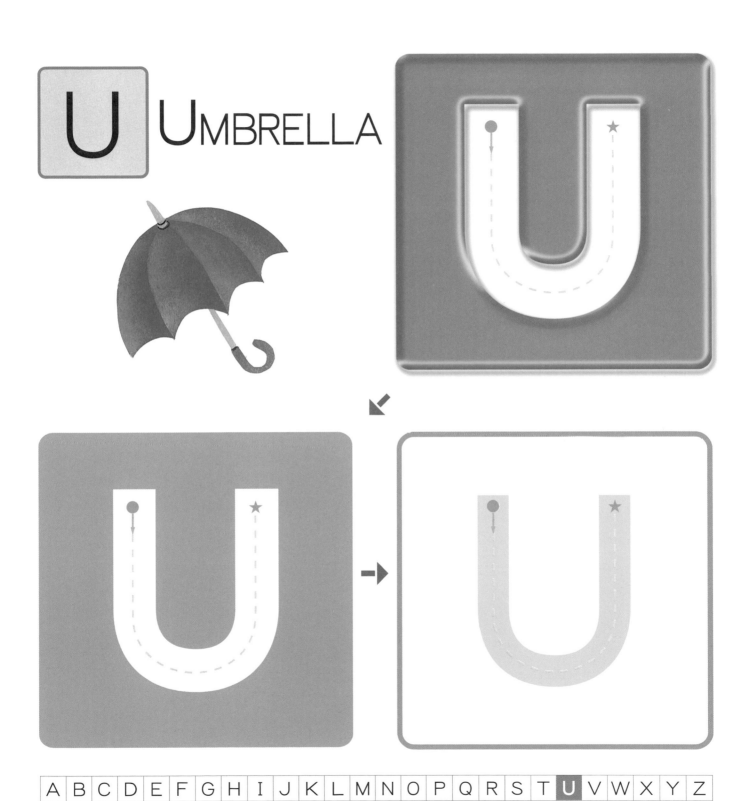

U UMBRELLA

| A | B | C | D | E | F | G | H | I | J | K | L | M | N | O | P | Q | R | S | T | U | V | W | X | Y | Z |

Writing R, J, and U

■ Draw a line from the dot(●) to the star(★).
Follow the order of the numbers.

Ring

Jam

Umbrella

■ Draw a line from the dot(●) to the star(★).
Follow the order of the numbers.

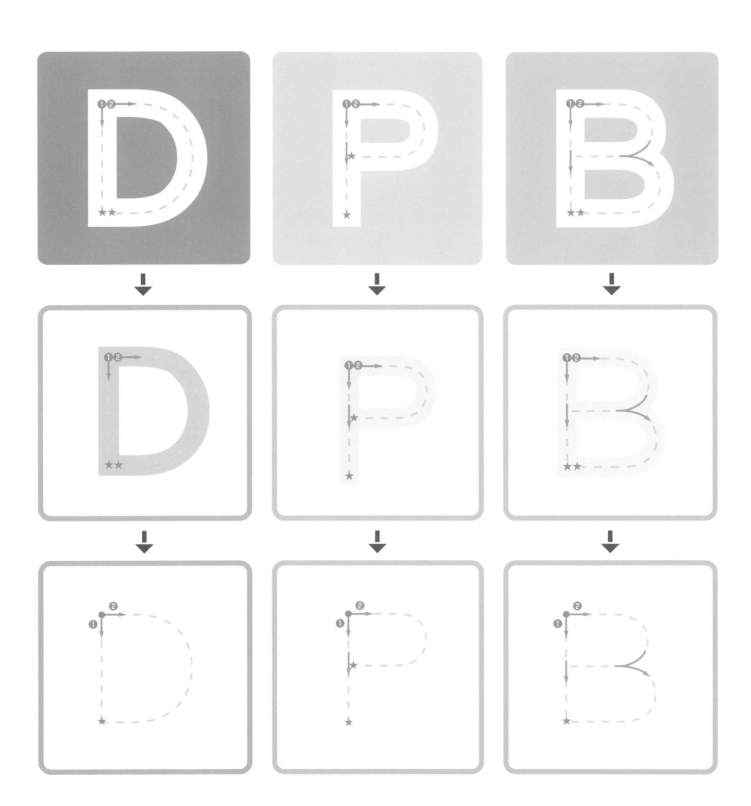

Writing R, J, and U

■ Draw a line from the dot(●) to the star(★).
Follow the order of the numbers.

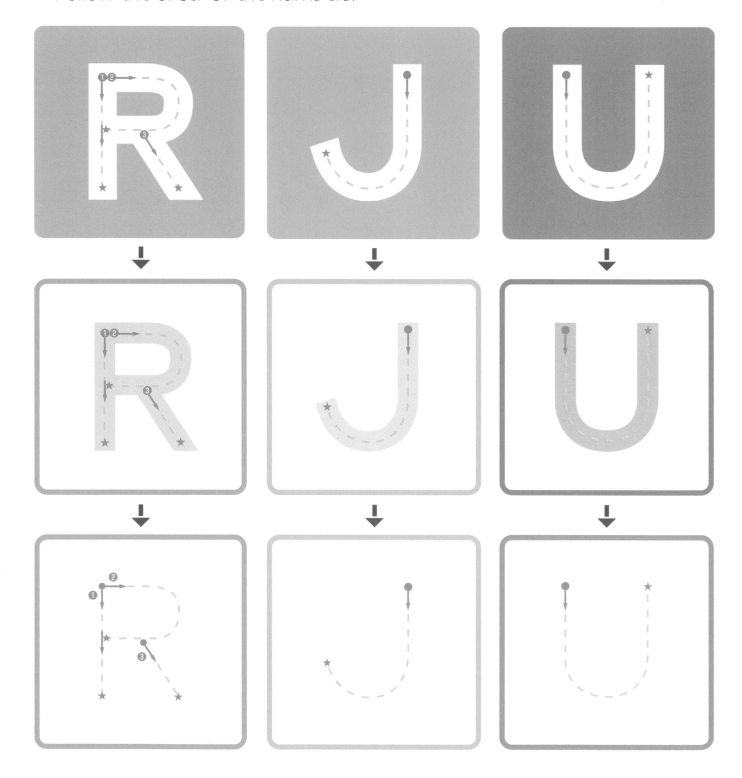

26 Drawing Wavy Lines

To parents: From this page on, your child will practice drawing wavy lines that will make up letters. Encourage your child to move his or her pencil slowly along the curved path.

■ Draw a line connecting each pair of pictures.

■ Draw a line connecting each pair of pictures.

Drawing Wavy Lines

■ Draw a line connecting each pair of pictures.

■ Draw a line connecting each pair of pictures.

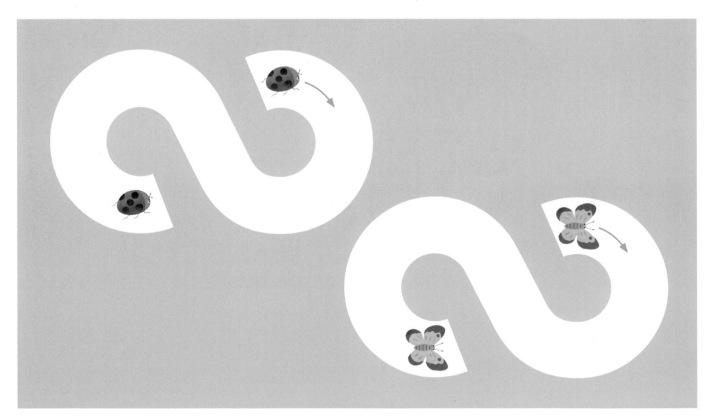

Drawing Circle Lines

Name

Date

/ /

To parents: It is okay if your child draws outside the white area. The important thing is to encourage your child to draw slowly and carefully.

■ Draw a line connecting each pair of pictures.

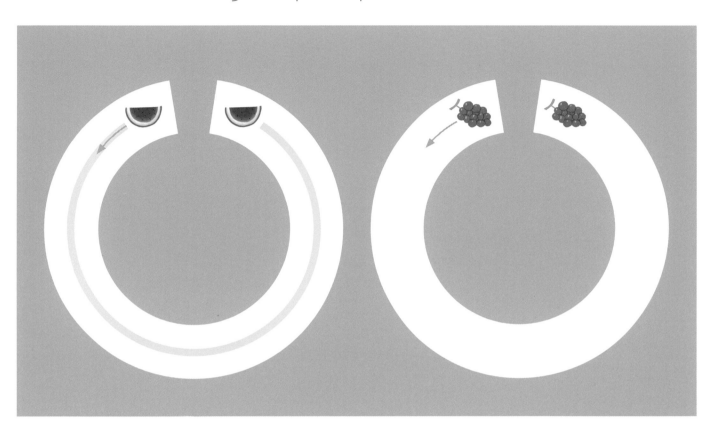

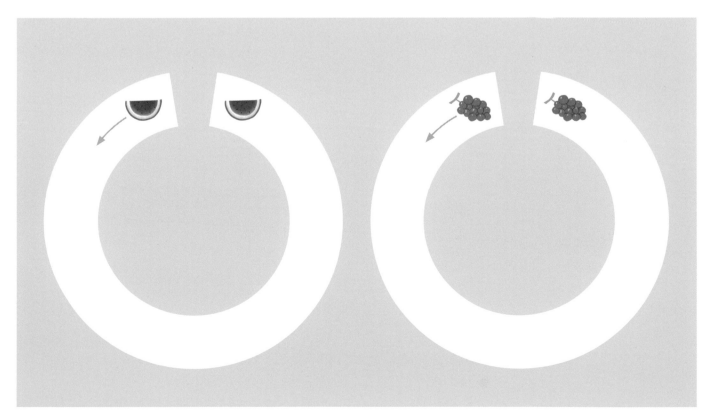

■ Draw a line connecting each pair of pictures.

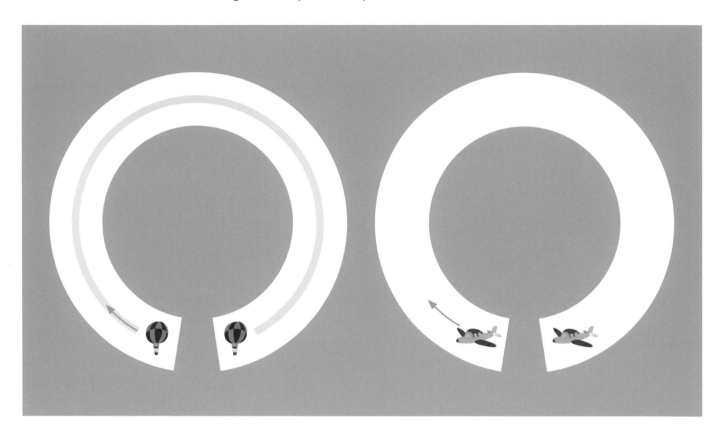

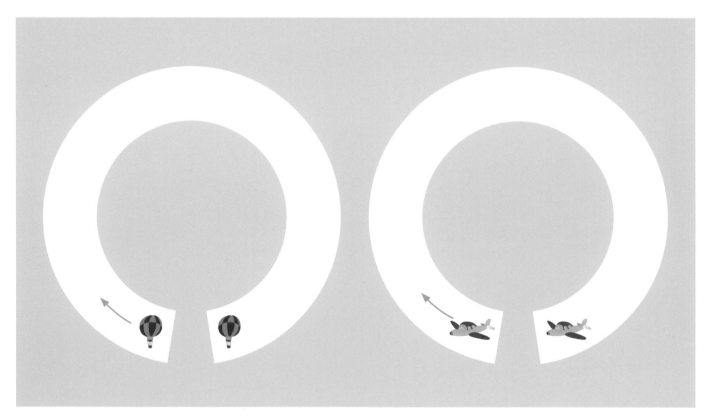

Drawing Circle Lines

Name

Date

/ /

■ Draw a line connecting each pair of pictures.

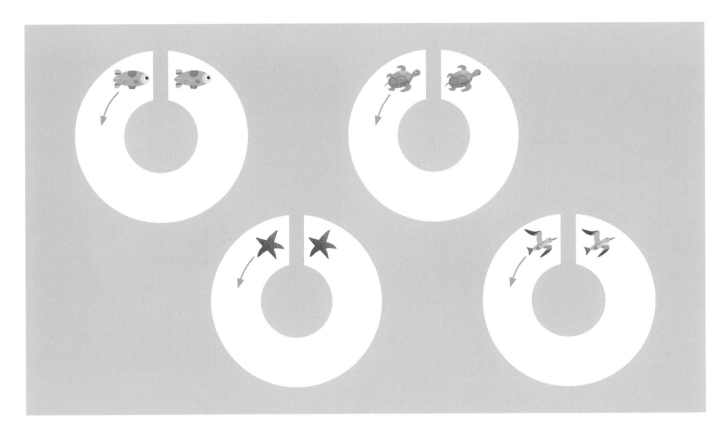

Writing C

■ Draw a line from the dot(●) to the star(★).

C **C**AT

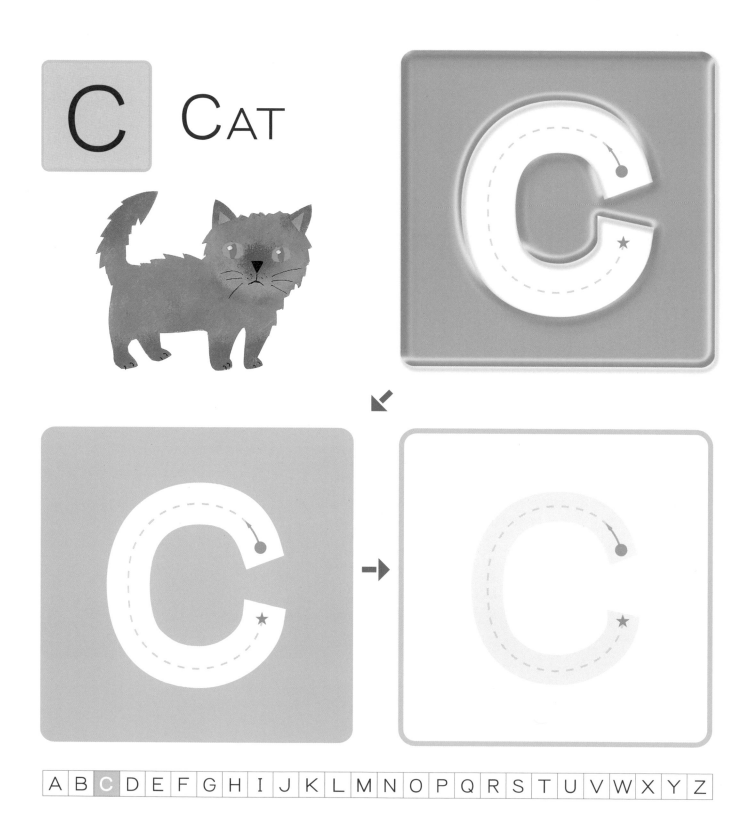

A B C D E F G H I J K L M N O P Q R S T U V W X Y Z

■ Draw a line from the dot(●) to the star(★).
Follow the order of the numbers.

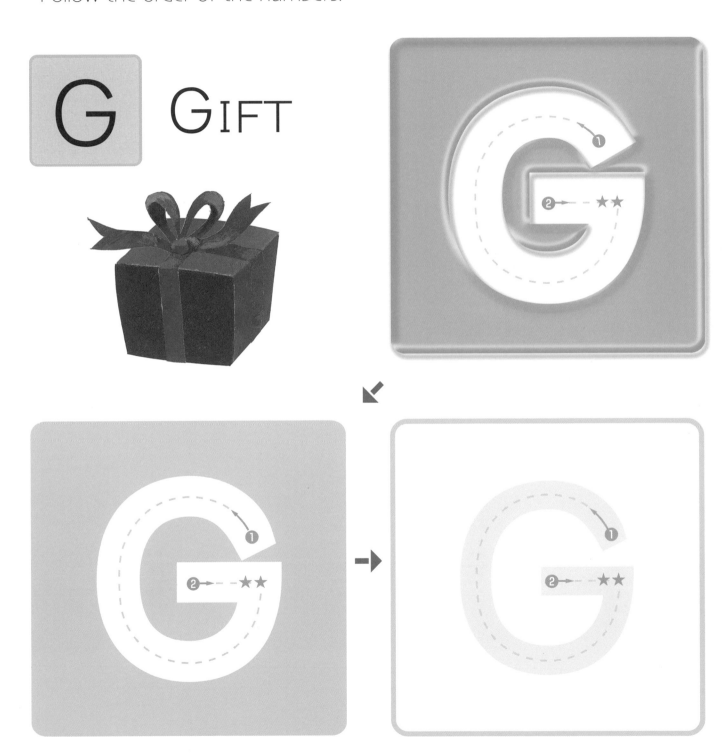

G GIFT

A B C D E F G H I J K L M N O P Q R S T U V W X Y Z

■ Draw a line from the dot(●) to the star(★).

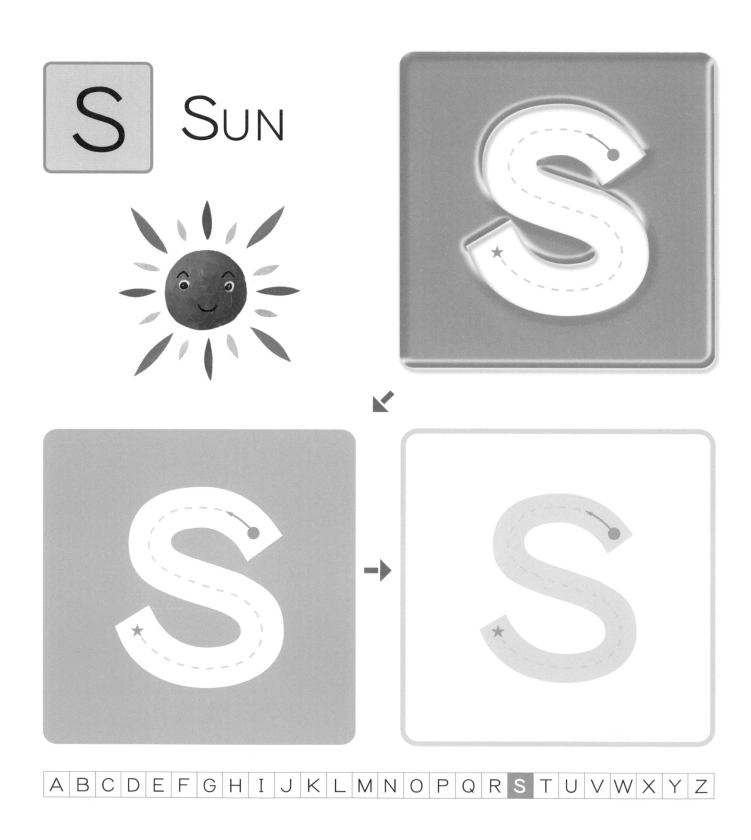

S SUN

A B C D E F G H I J K L M N O P Q R **S** T U V W X Y Z

Tracing Letters
Writing C, G, and S

■ Draw a line from the dot(●) to the star(★).
Follow the order of the numbers.

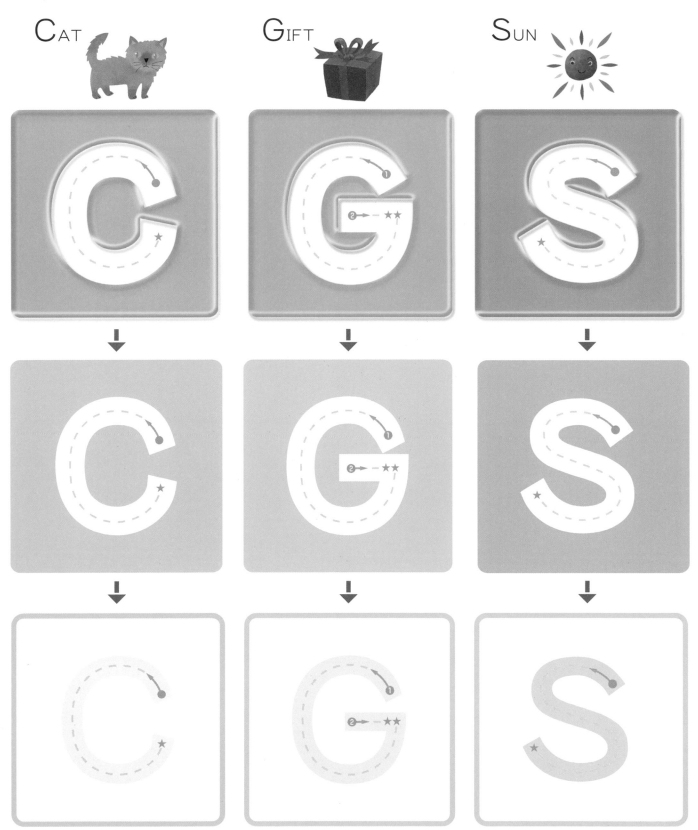

C<small>AT</small>

G<small>IFT</small>

S<small>UN</small>

Writing O

■ Draw a line from the dot(●) to the star(★).

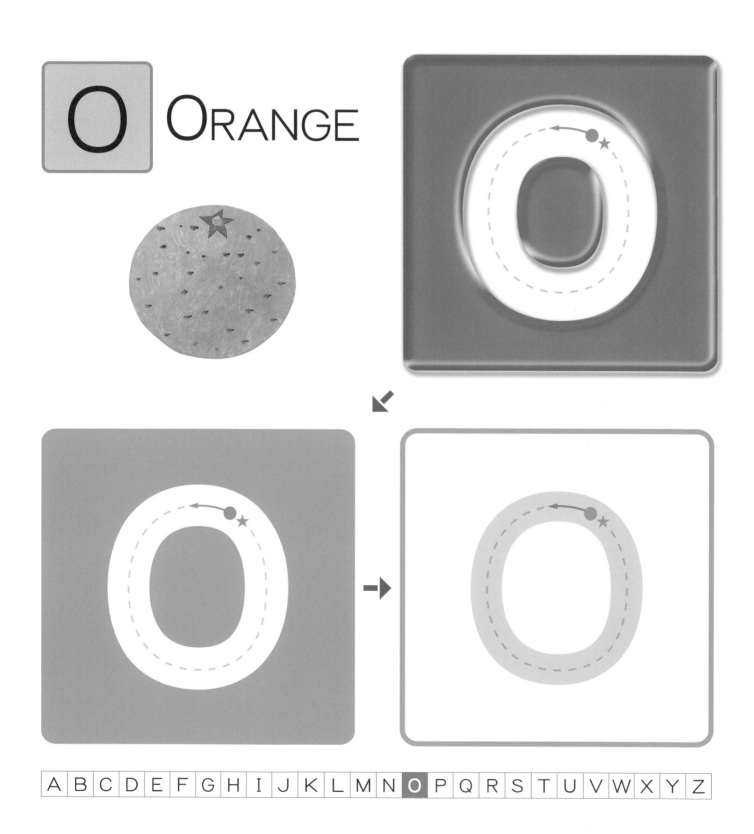

O ORANGE

■ Draw a line from the dot(●) to the star(★).
Follow the order of the numbers.

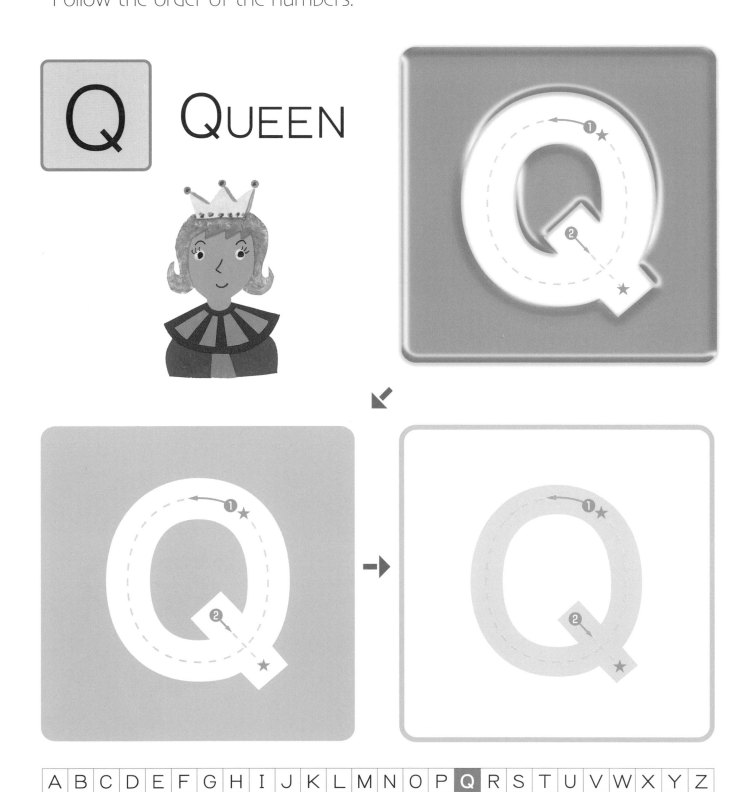

Q QUEEN

| A | B | C | D | E | F | G | H | I | J | K | L | M | N | O | P | Q | R | S | T | U | V | W | X | Y | Z |

Writing O and Q

■ Draw a line from the dot(●) to the star(★).
Follow the order of the numbers.

ORANGE QUEEN

Review
Writing C, G, and S

Name

Date

/ /

■ Draw a line from the dot(●) to the star(★).
Follow the order of the numbers.

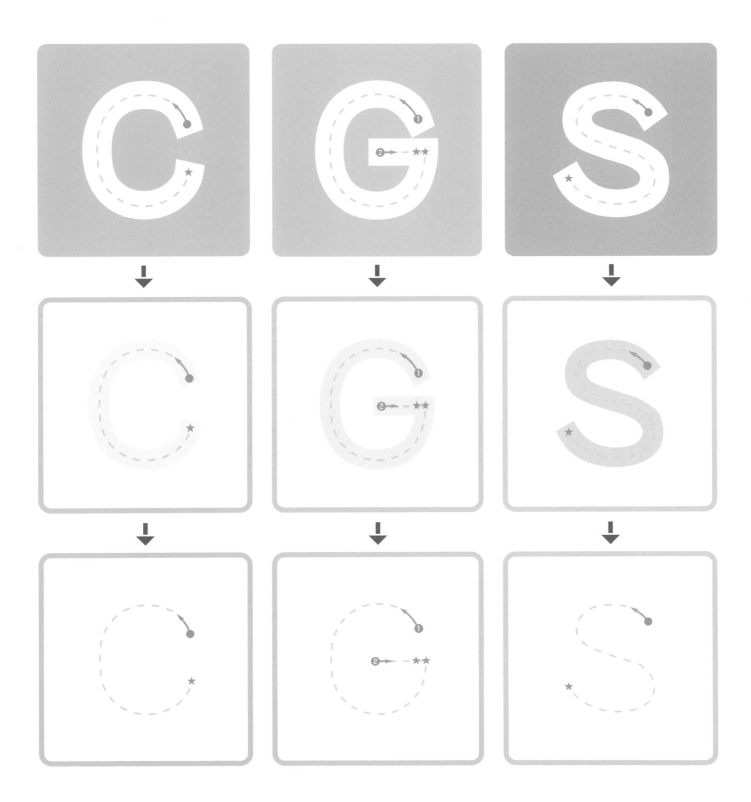

Writing O and Q

■ Draw a line from the dot(●) to the star(★).
  Follow the order of the numbers.

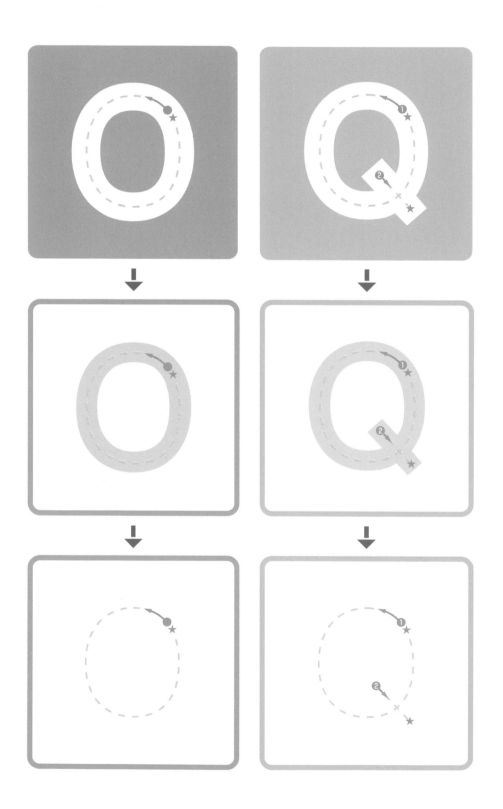

Name

Date

■ Trace the letters below.

Writing A, B, and C

To parents: From this page on, your child will review all the letters in alphabetical order. Encourage him or her to write slowly and carefully. When your child has completed the exercise, offer lots of praise.

■ Draw a line from the dot(●) to the star(★).
Follow the order of the numbers.

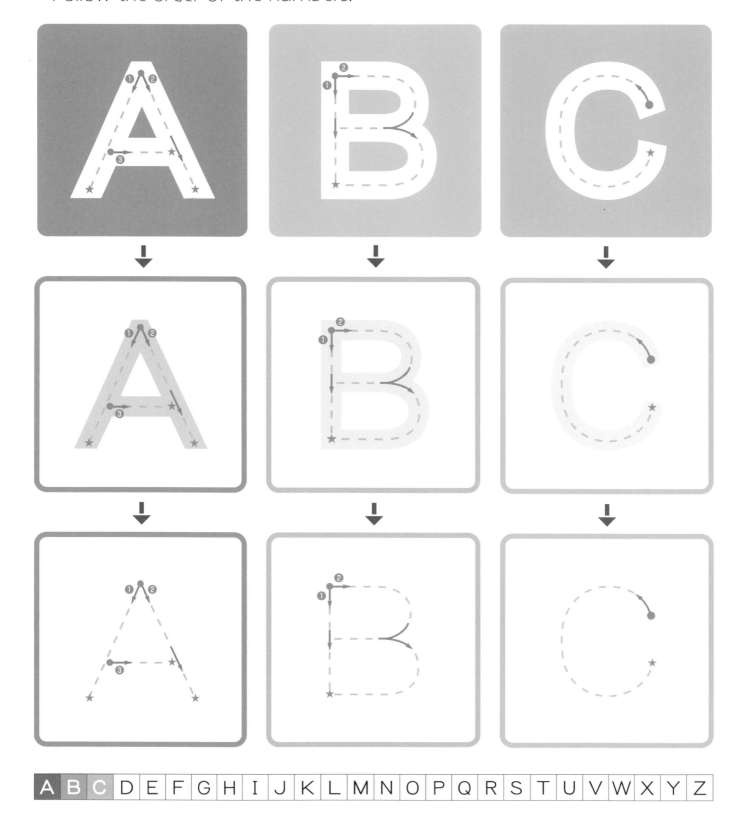

| A | B | C | D | E | F | G | H | I | J | K | L | M | N | O | P | Q | R | S | T | U | V | W | X | Y | Z |

Review
Writing D, E, and F

■ Draw a line from the dot(●) to the star(★).
 Follow the order of the numbers.

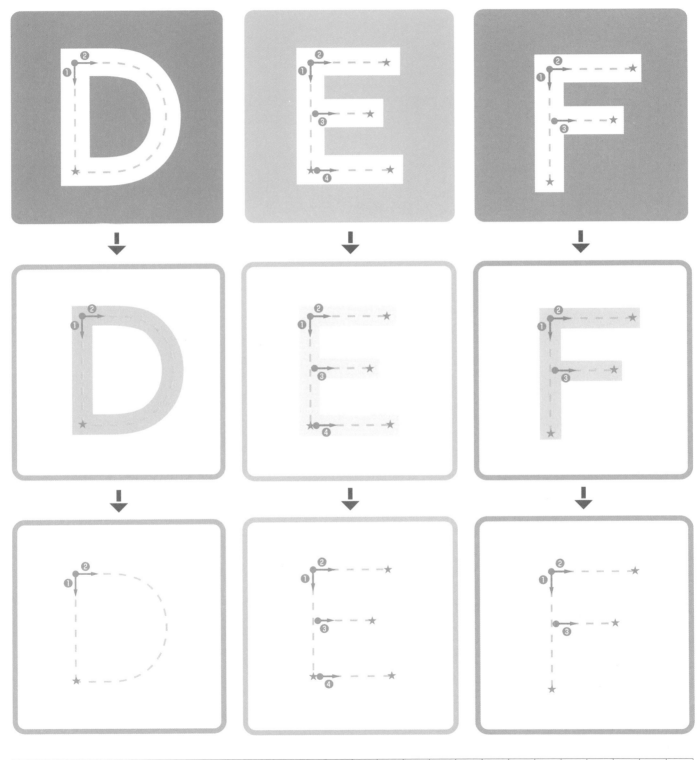

A B C **D E F** G H I J K L M N O P Q R S T U V W X Y Z

Writing G, H, and I

■ Draw a line from the dot(●) to the star(★).
  Follow the order of the numbers.

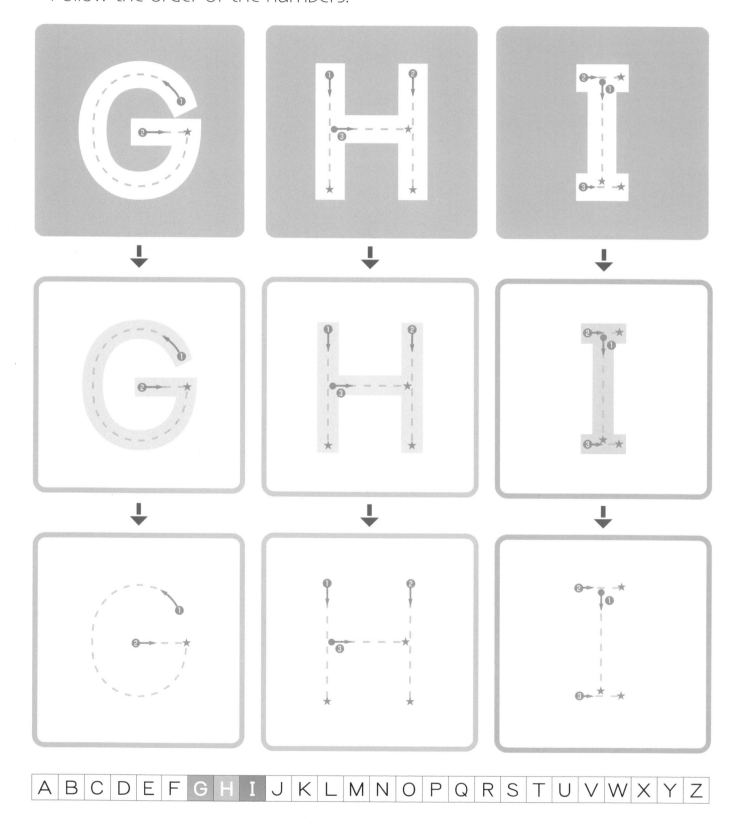

■ Draw a line from the dot(●) to the star(★).
  Follow the order of the numbers.

A B C D E F G H I **J K L** M N O P Q R S T U V W X Y Z

Writing M, N, and O

■ Draw a line from the dot(●) to the star(★).
Follow the order of the numbers.

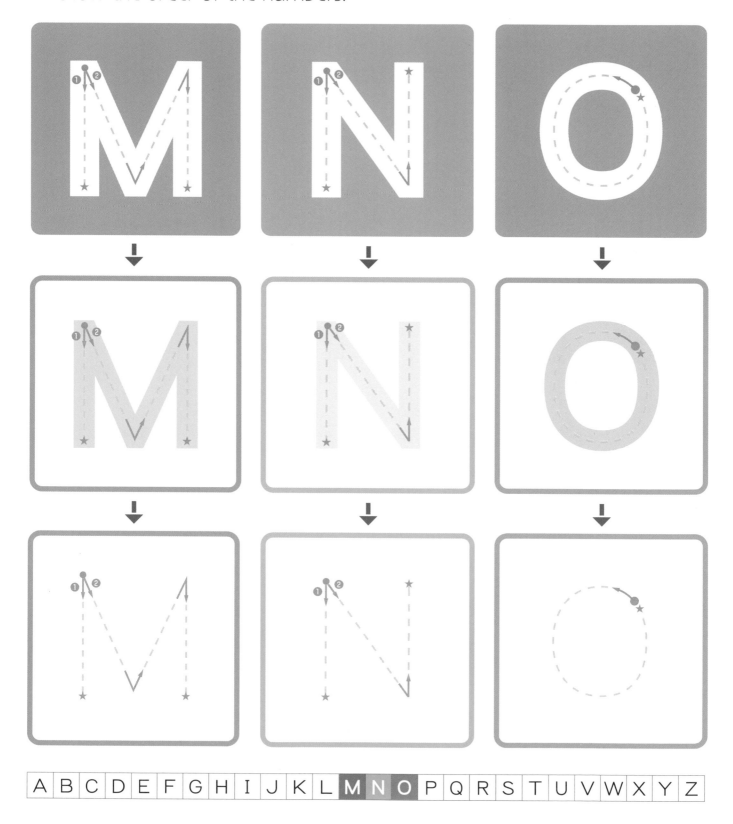

■ Draw a line from the dot(●) to the star(★).
Follow the order of the numbers.

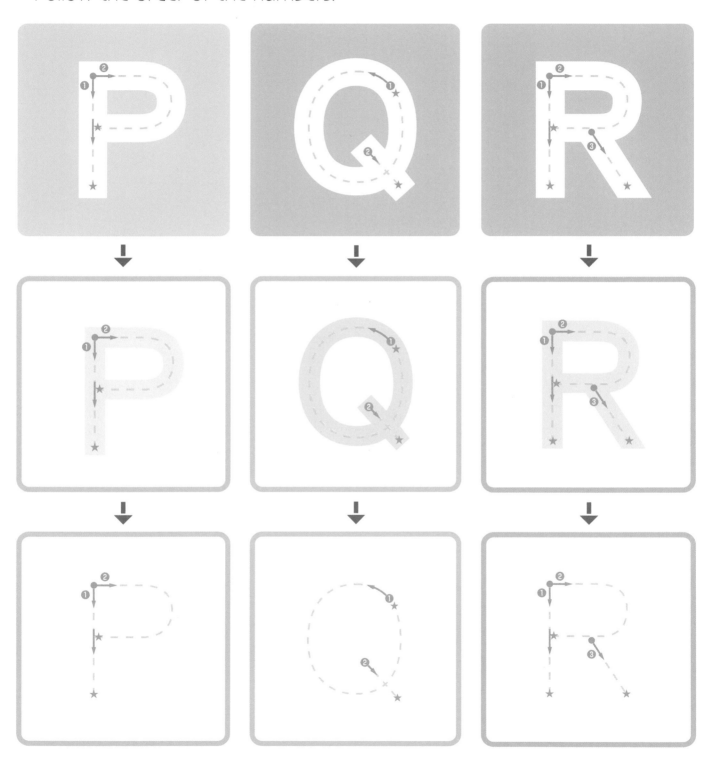

| A | B | C | D | E | F | G | H | I | J | K | L | M | N | O | P | Q | R | S | T | U | V | W | X | Y | Z |

Writing S, T, and U

■ Draw a line from the dot(●) to the star(★).
Follow the order of the numbers.

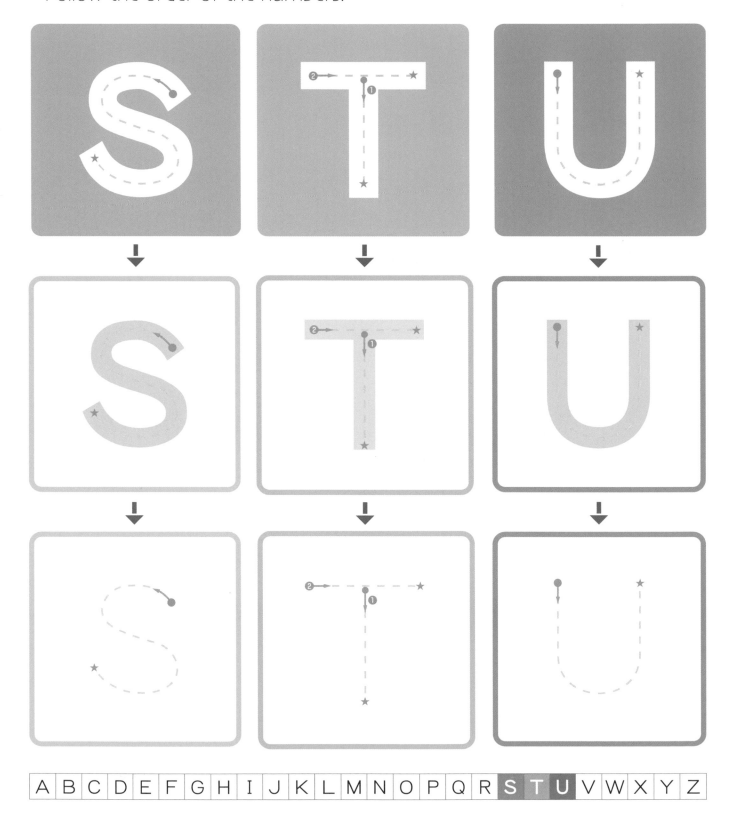

Review
Writing V, W, and X

■ Draw a line from the dot(●) to the star(★).
Follow the order of the numbers.

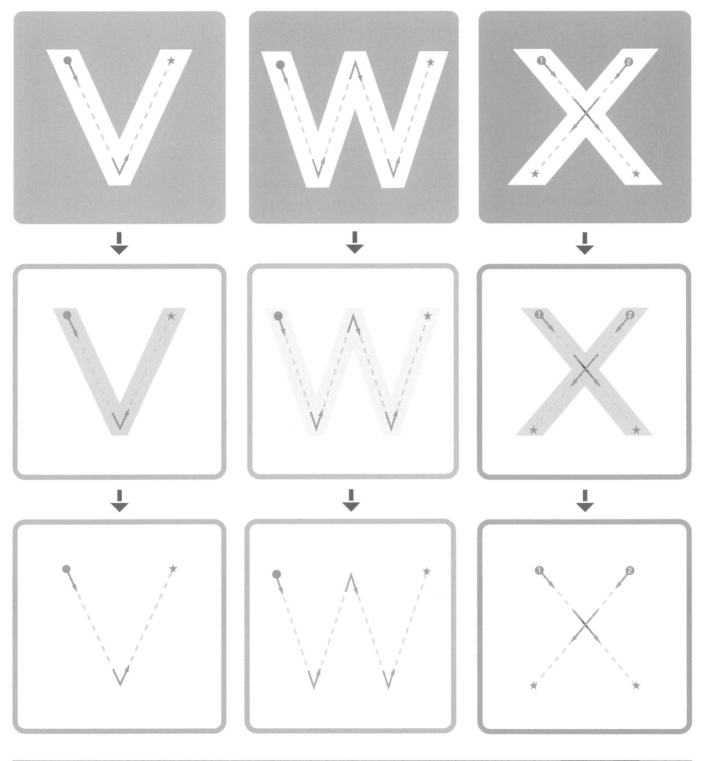

| A | B | C | D | E | F | G | H | I | J | K | L | M | N | O | P | Q | R | S | T | U | V | W | X | Y | Z |

Writing Y and Z

■ Draw a line from the dot(●) to the star(★).
Follow the order of the numbers.

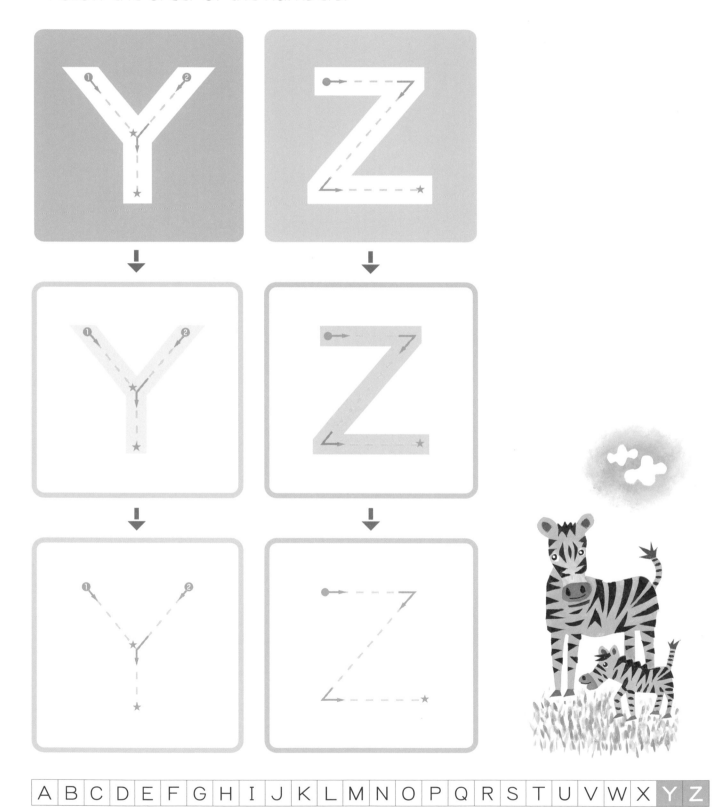

Name   Date
/   /

To parents: When your child has finished this book, give him or her the Certificate of Achievement on which you can write his or her name and the date. Give your child lots of praise for his or her effort!

■ Trace the letters A to Z.

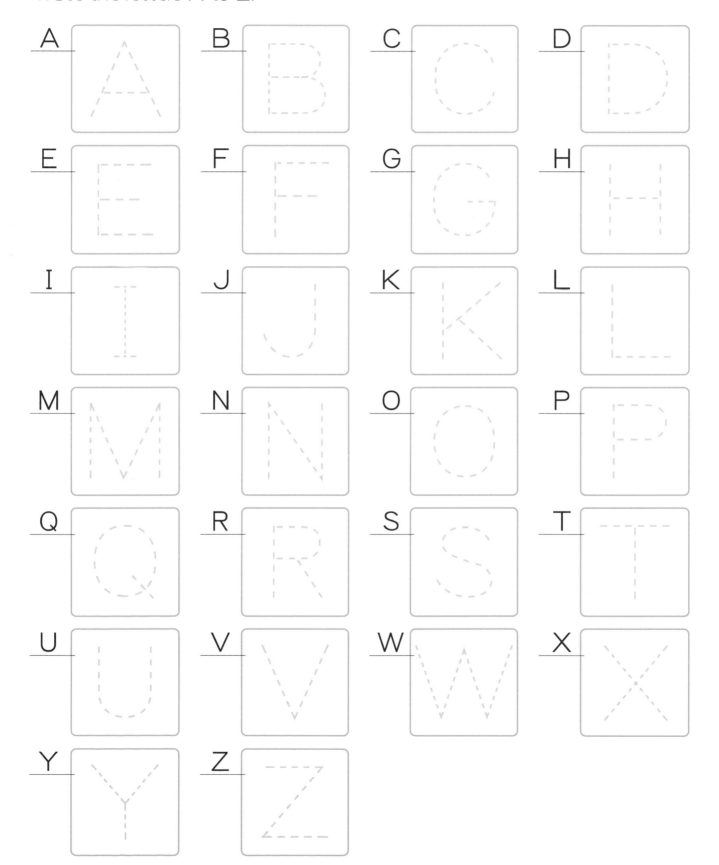

Writing A-Z

■ Write the letters A to Z, as shown on the left.

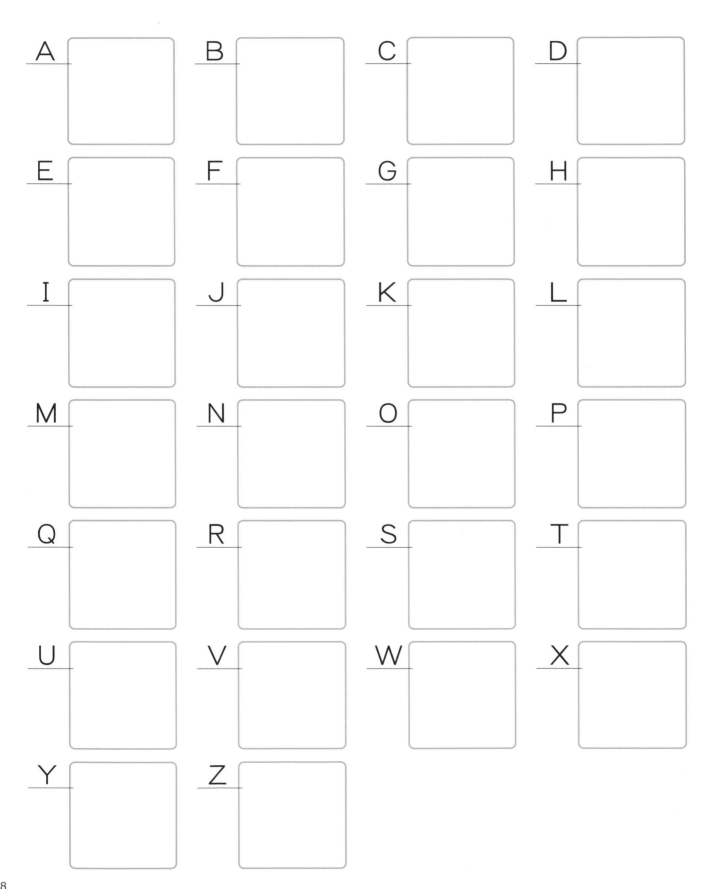

A

B

C

D

E

F

G

H

I

J

K

L

M

N

O

P

Q

R

S

T

U

V

W

X

Y

Z

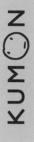

Certificate of Achievement

_____

is hereby congratulated on completing

My Book of Uppercase Letters

Presented on _____ , 20 _____

_____

Parent or Guardian